BRENDAN CORBETT

THE
THIEF
AND THE
HISTORIAN

BOOK ONE OF THE RUNETREE CHRONICLES

Editor: Djuna Faye Whistler

Illustrator: Tom Edwards

TomEdwardsDesign.com

The Thief and the Historian / Brendan Corbett
ISBN: 978-1-949813-36-4

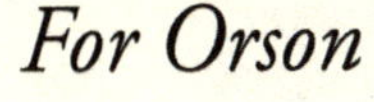

For Orson

CHAPTER

ONE

Dusk settled over the coastal city of Biersport. All was silent, except for the sweep of gentle waves by the piers. Residents had long been asleep, awaiting night-fishing ships that would arrive at dawn. Moonlight spilled over the city save the Cliff District, nestled beneath a towering rock outcropping. In this darkness, a man strutted towards a shop with shoddy walls and a window of small squares of thick glass. He approached as a single candle burned low within. A wooden sign dangling from a thick iron nail in the door advertised the apothecary "OPEN" in faded black ink.

The man shoved the door open and stepped into the dim, one-room store. His short, ratty leather boots with obnoxiously large buckles clicked with each step until he paused to brush dust from his fancy coat, all tattered. He chuckled as he made eye contact with the shopkeeper, a large fellow slouched behind a pockmarked counter.

The visitor flipped the door sign around, displaying "CLOSED". His jagged teeth crept out from behind narrow lips, forming a smug smile beneath his hooked nose.

"If you'll please," came the gravelly voice of the shopkeeper, his cheek twitching in irritation.

"If I'll please, what?" Replied the man, halting mid-step.

"If you'll please, Braedyn, you'll flip that sign back 'round or you might find yourself having an accident on the way to your meeting. We are *open*."

The visitor's smile fell, replaced by a leer. Without turning, he reached back to flip the sign with a calloused finger before resuming his walk to the rear of the shop, the sign chattering behind. He passed tightly staged rows of shelves, packed with bottles and jars filled with an endless variety of leaves and seeds and other less easily identifiable ingredients. Slipping through a passageway at the back wall, he descended a stairway to a cellar crowded with wooden barrels large enough to hold sheep. In the dark, the air cool and stale, he ducked behind a container of acrid-smelling oil. Bringing his heel down on a lever, he pushed open a secret panel in the wall.

The room glowed a dull yellow. Men and women sat around a broad table. Biersport natives, all. They had dark curly hair with skin tanned and tough from years beneath sun and within coastal winds, and wore loose linen shirts and pants dyed in pale tans, greens, and blues. Braedyn, ever the outsider, stood apart. He had never cared to conform to the typical Biersport dress.

He recognized many of his fellow Stewards from the Grey Society. While their title marked them as peers, to him, they stood beneath his ambitions. Conversation ceased upon his arrival.

How could these simpletons be capable of managing and directing Thieves? He mused. *How far has the Council lowered their standards?*

"Hello, friends," he sneered, taking a seat at one end of the table. The others turned away, resuming their conversations. Braedyn leaned back in his chair, feet on the table.

Two people strode in from a door at the opposite end of the room. They wore long, hooded grey cloaks, with a belt of small pouches encircling their waists. As they neared the table, candlelight illuminated their intricate rose-red masks, adorned in gold stitching. The room became still as death as the Stewards stared into the newcomers' eyes.

"You have been called here today for a unique opportunity," came a man's calm, yet commanding, voice. "The Society requires something far greater than a trinket from a common mark. The one who retrieves this will find their life forever changed."

"The Council has deemed each of you to be of sufficient quality," followed a woman with a sweet voice, like overripe berries. "As such, you will have equal opportunity to vie for this prize."

Braedyn noticed the corners of her eyes crease gleefully as the Stewards murmured amongst themselves. They had been made to contend against each other before, of course, but never so many at once.

A Steward broke the hushed conversation and pointed a bulbous finger at Braedyn. "You said quality. What's he doing here!?" the man spewed and spat as if caramel filled his mouth. "That fool don't know the first thing about acquisition. He does nothing but poach from us honest gentlemen and ladies. Why is he here?!"

The Stewards found their voices, muttering disdainfully

about Braedyn's underhanded tactic of directing his Thief to steal from other Thieves rather than directly from a mark. Braedyn offered a toothy smirk in reply.

"Quiet, Jeobinas," said the woman, cutting through the din like a sword through paper. "If you believe yourself to be so great as to decide who should be present, then perhaps you are above this meeting."

Jeobinas and the other Stewards shrank in silence. Braedyn's grin spread as the second Attendant continued. "Braedyn's methods might be unorthodox, but they are not in violation of the Society's creed. He was included by the Council's judgement, which is a satisfactory answer to your question. Now, if you all have finished voicing what little thought fills your simple heads, then we will proceed with meaningful discussion. Tomorrow, at midday, a Historian will arrive in Biersport. You are tasked with stealing her life essences."

Braedyn's smile drooped into a grimace. Even for the Grey Society, which directed Stewards and their Thieves to steal from dignitaries and royalty without discrimination, theft from a Historian was bold.

"Pick up your jaws and open your ears. We have much to discuss."

Gathering close, the Stewards listened intently as the night wore on, eagerly seeking morsels of information

Like chicks in a bird's nest waiting for worms from their mother, Braedyn thought to himself, eyeing his compatriots. *If only they had such a Thief as my Aeda, they might have some confidence in their odds of success. She may be half the age of many Thieves, but she has twice the skill. I will be the victor in this!*

Shortly before dawn, they scurried from the shop into the drab morning to find their Thieves.

Jeobinas bolted through the city. He paused, doubled over, to compose himself near a gate in the city wall. Still wheezing, he sidled up to a rigid man with a curled brown beard and held out a pouch of coins. The man took the offering with a hand absent its pointer finger. Upon examining the contents, his shoulders relaxed, and the two spoke in whispers.

A fleck of dust settled on the tip of Aeda's eyelashes and her eyes fluttered open. A feeble ray of light shone over her in the early morning darkness. To her side, the floor abruptly ended. A torrent of water gushed by in a culvert a few feet below, its rumbling filling her ears.

She stretched on her thin mat, sending bracelets clinking down her arm. She had made them herself, of shells and barnacles and strands of scavenged sailor's rope; their gentle sound comforted her. She cinched her billowy pants around her waist with a plaited cord and stepped into woven rope shoes. Though the footwear looked meager, its worn threads were soft and pliable. She yawned into a snug sleeveless shirt, then flipped her satchel over her shoulder.

She filled a cup from the surging culvert and drank deeply. Refreshed and alert, she scaled a metal ladder beneath the stream of light. At the last rung, she turned a plum-sized metal orb in the wall. Above her, a grate made of interlocked metal flaps opened like a blossoming flower. Sweet, salty air rushed in and goosebumps raced across her arms as she exited the cistern. She twisted another metal orb embedded in the ground to close the grate behind her.

Aeda spilled out from the alley into a street on a hill, where she could see the ocean over the rooftops of Biersport while the sun painted the horizon in swaths of pink and yellow. She groggily trudged towards the market, her stomach churning in protest of the cold drink with no food to follow. Focused on sating her appetite, the girl all but ignored her surroundings.

The city was waking; the sounds of doors creaking open and yawns spread through the streets. Clusters of two-story buildings stood between brown cobblestone streets, with tan and grey sand packed between the pavers. Designed with care, the thick, sandy concrete walls of the buildings had rounded corners to ease the burden of storms. Dark green, maroon, and purple trims laced windows and doors, colored with dyes from ocean plants. Most windows were open holes with wooden shutters; thin glass was too brittle to endure hurricanes, while thick glass was too expensive for all but the wealthiest to afford.

Towers of four stout wooden poles punctuated the streets, supporting platforms high above. Running between the towers were wooden channels which crossed back and forth, filled with water like floating rivers. Skiffs sped through the channels, hauling goods across the city.

A shop door banged open, its frame quivering. A delectable aroma crept out, and Aeda's belly grumbled as she eyed egg-washed breads, frosted cakes, and sweet pastries lining the window. She dug into her satchel, retrieving a few small rectangles of stamped copper. Her eyes pored over every pock, dent, and scratch on the coins, counting the meager sum with disdain. *Three nails, not even a finger's worth.* Sighing, Aeda balled her fist and pulled away from the tempting treats.

The Grand Plaza hosted dozens of shopkeepers, pushing their brightly painted carts into place. They hurriedly unfurled canvas covers and set their wares out for viewing, as early market goers arrived. Aeda approached a stall near the edge, her knuckles growing white as she tightened her clutch on her coins.

A hefty man with a bushy mustache and a greeted her as she arrived. "Well hello, Aeda," he said, whiskers flickering with each word of his mellow voice. He leaned over his cart and whispered as she toyed with the nails. "Might be time to see Mr. Braedyn, hm?"

Aeda's brow furrowed. She knew he was right, though did not appreciate the need to see her Steward again. As she reached for a dried fish, a hand flew out and clasped tightly over her wrist. Aeda flinched, though the jacket cuff sporting colorful stitching immediately revealed its owner. Composing herself, she offered a feeble, disinterested smile to Braedyn. His eyes flicked back and forth between Aeda and the cart.

In a flurry, he stuffed food from the stall into her satchel, drawing protests from the shopkeeper. Aeda joined in complaint, though her words were tepid as her stomach growled at the sight of food filling her satchel.

Braedyn's voice screeched with excitement. "Aeda, Aeda, Aeda, I have been looking for you! We have much to discuss, so much to discuss… Come, we need to talk somewhere less…

in this plaza."

Braedyn shoveled dried fish, fruits, vegetables, and miniature loaves of sweet bread into the satchel until nothing more could fit, then pulled away. The shopkeeper blustered his objections, raising his voice and reddening at the theft of his produce. Braedyn pacified the shopkeeper by rudely throwing a handful of nails and fingers of copper onto the cart before darting into the crowd.

Aeda fought to keep her satchel shut as Braedyn wove through the streets, back and forth, as if to lose an imaginary pursuer. He ducked into an alley behind a long-abandoned home, one of the Grey Society's safe houses, and released Aeda. Braedyn rested one hand on her shoulder while the other hand went about relieving her bulging satchel, tucking fruits and vegetables into his pockets. Aeda, unsurprised by his display of self-serving behavior, crossed her arms.

Braedyn caught his breath and stared into her eyes. "There is an opportunity made available to us, the kind of opportunity that may never come again."

What could this be if not another Braedyn tale of grandeur? Aeda slouched in disinterest. The Steward leaned in uncomfortably close and continued with urgency. "Just last night, this morning even, I was in a meeting with a dozen Stewards, led by no less than two Attendants. They have given us a new mark. A mark like none before. Aeda, my dear, the Council has tasked us with stealing rune essences from a Historian."

He paused with his hands raised, awaiting a joyful response. To his disappointment, Aeda was entirely unaffected. "I forget you aren't exactly educated," he said flatly. "As you know, we live in the wonderful city of Biersport, finest city in all the Known Lands. Now, the Historians are a group of people who constantly roam, recording history in giant books they carry at their side. The gods themselves decreed this writing of history, meaning Historians are more important than any dignitary or merchant or noble. Not only is this Historian an exceedingly rare mark, when I successfully steal from one, it will earn me unimaginable fame in the Society."

"Ahem," Aeda cleared her throat, staring at Braedyn, his pompous finger pointing to the sky and eyes glossed. She was more bothered by his interest in taking credit for her work than she was by his patronizing tone. "Don't you mean if I successfully steal from this Historian? Or perhaps you plan to join me this time?"

"Steward and Thief are one and the same," he replied sourly. "Moving on, essences are used for runewriting. You've seen the Attendants; they carry rune essence in the pouches on their belts. The Historian has five pouches for essence on her belt. You'll need to figure out which one has the life essence. They are purple. The Attendants say it's most likely the pouch furthest from the Historian's belt buckle, but there's no guarantee."

"If the Attendants already have life essences, why do we need to steal more from this Historian?"

"Because the Council asked us to. That should be enough for you," Braedyn chided.

Aeda remained cautious, yet resigned to complete the task. "When will the Historian arrive?"

"She'll be here today. Soon, I would think. Perhaps in a few hours. Apparently, she prefers to loiter in markets when she arrives. You should wait for her at the Grand Plaza."

"We were just in the Grand Plaza."

"So, you'll go back there now. Oh, and you will retrieve the essence today. The other Stewards and Thieves will take time to observe and form their plots, but they will not delay for long. This is too important to risk another Thief taking the mark first, no time for us to wait and plan. Also, there is no Fence; we are to take these essences directly to an Attendant. I'll find you after you acquire the essences and then we'll report together in the evening. Remember, when we succeed, the reward will be beyond dreams!"

"But…" Braedyn turned and shuffled out of the alley, dismissively waving his hand. "Typical," Aeda muttered and worked her way back through the city. *Why even have a Steward if all he does is dream? Not even the slightest bit of insight into what I should do.*

The sun had risen barely above the horizon, yet people flooded the streets. Avoiding the main avenues, Aeda coasted through shadowy alleys until she emerged at a ledge overlooking the Grand Plaza. Sitting on the perch, she watched market-goers flowing down the main avenue. The Thief hoped a plan might come to her before the Historian arrived, though her mind wandered as the sun climbed, glowing warmly above. She rearranged the remaining food in her satchel and munched on a sweet oat roll.

Pulled from her daydream, she tensed upon seeing an unusually dressed woman strolling towards the market. While merchants from various parts of the Known Lands were common enough in Biersport, this woman's appearance was distinct.

She wore dark brown boots which rose halfway up her calf, the mud-flecked leather slicked with oil and trimmed in steel rings. Her pants were a grey muslin, with leather pads stitched over the knees and thighs. Leather pauldrons ran halfway down her upper arm, and vambraces capped her sleeves at her wrists. A deep red tabard sat over a burnt orange linen shirt, emblazoned with a white tome over a tree, tucked into a thick leather belt sporting a row of small pouches. A second belt was home to a sword, the weapon imposing even though sheathed. A leather-bound tome hanging from a fine silver chain at the woman's right hip confirmed that she was a Historian.

I might as well go for it now. Aeda pushed off from the ledge and into the crowd.

CHAPTER

TWO

The morning sun was pleasantly warm as Gieral ambled along a stone-paved road. A powerful roan horse and a grey mule followed close behind, neither of which had a lead rope. The mule pulled a four-wheeled cart piled high with provisions, its wooden rails aged and smooth like rocks in a riverbed.

The trio crested a knoll above a field of rolling hills covered in golden wheat. Workers roamed the landscape, harvesting the crop and loading it into wide-mouthed baskets slung on their backs. The road sloped gently down to the coast, where the high walls of Biersport were visible, flanked by cliffs. Gieral thought fondly of the markets inside the city, where visiting merchants would haggle and barter. She had a mind to visit the docks, where a flurry of workers swarmed like ants to unload fishing and merchant ships alike.

As Gieral continued towards Biersport, fine sand replaced the packed brown earth that filled gaps between stones. A squashed hodgepodge of crude inns and stables built atop each other crowded the main city gate. Merchants crammed by the entryway as the sun rose in the sky. A second gate, its use only permitted for citizens of Biersport, was tranquil.

The Historian lodged her horse and mule at a stable, leaving each with a sweet purple carrot. Nearing the gate, Gieral passed a storehouse, where merchants deposited their wares in exchange for cloth tickets. With these tickets in hand, merchants would enter Biersport unburdened by their goods, free to roam and trade in the city. Residents of Biersport traded for the cloth tickets and returned them to counting houses to receive their due.

The Historian waded into the cacophonous mass by the gate, where long, tapered crimson banners curled and twisted in the ocean breeze. The stifling smell of sweat filled her nose as she pressed through the crowd. Merchants pushed and prodded, swirling like an eddy in a tidal pool, trying to hasten their way in. Guards stood sentry at the gates and recorded entrances in ledgers, openly taking bribes to expedite entry. Gieral worked her way forward, patiently waiting until a pair of guards motioned her over.

The guards wore bronze helmets that spiraled up from their necks and around their heads like a shell. Their armor moved like scales, stiff leather squares linked with hoops of metal and trimmed in maroon thread. It hung over billowy and loose almond-colored pants tucked into short leather shoes. The first guard, sporting a thick black mustache, held a ledger and a quill. The second twisted the end of a taut braid, a hand resting on the hilt of a narrow-bladed sword.

"You don't have to wait. Historians can go directly through," the guard with the ledger droned, motioning her by with his quill. His eyes darted away from Gieral and into the crowd, looking for the next merchant to call.

The Historian stood squarely in front of him and spoke with words warm, yet measured. "My name is Gieral of the Moor, mark of the White Crane."

The guard's face pursed. He raised the ledger, writing feverishly with his quill while staring at Gieral.

She had a small braid on either side of her face tied back with the rest of her wavy brown hair. Her nose had most certainly been broken in the past, framed by tall cheekbones and a wide jaw. Deeply set silver-grey eyes looked with an aged experience of one who lived a storied life.

"Name… Gieral… place of origin… the Moor. And what is your reason for coming to Biersport, my dear Historian?" The guard said, his words laden with sarcasm.

"That's Gieral of the Moor, *Mark of the White Crane*. I am here to commune with the Runetree. I expect to be in Biersport for no more than a week."

The guard hastily highlighted her line in the ledger and clamped it shut. "Right, fine, done, perfect, off you are. Thank you, then!"

Gieral offered a shallow bow then passed through the gate. Unnoticed by her, another guard had slipped away from his post. Reaching into a wooden cage, he tied a rolled note to a pigeon's leg. The guard balanced the bird on his middle finger beside the nub of his pointer, releasing it then resuming his sentry.

Gieral drank in a refreshing breeze of sweet and salty air upon entering Biersport. The pure blue ocean filled the space between rooftops and the horizon, nearly blending into the sky. The four tiers of the city sprawled before her, with avenues leading down a gentle slope from the walls to the docks. Each level was wide enough to hold three paved boulevards lined with houses and stores and factories. Overhead channels ignored the well-planned streets, crossing over buildings like kite strings caught in tree branches. In the distance was the Cliff District, the oldest section of the city and an exception to the orderly structure, largely forgotten and shaded for most of the day.

Residents filled the streets while merchants brandishing cloth tickets sought buyers for their wares. Skiffs sloshed in the overhead channels and the docks were abuzz as fishers unloaded the day's catch from their ships. The weather begged for a leisurely stroll, which Gieral indulged, heading to the Grand Plaza in the heart of the city. Stalls and carts with bright canopies lined the avenue, displaying goods from fresh fish to fruits, woven clothing to rough furs, jewels to pottery, and more. Stores with colorful banners had their doors propped wide open to invite customers in while stall workers beckoned, tempting passersby at every turn.

The street opened as Gieral rounded a bend, giving way to the Grand Plaza, filled with dozens of stalls. Shoppers swarmed within, swirling like sand with the tide. A thin and disheveled girl sitting on an embankment above the market drew Gieral's attention. While everyone in sight was preoccupied with buying or selling or some other pressing task, this girl leaned back almost idly, yet her eyes sharply observed the market.

Gieral joined the market throng, cautiously watching as the girl sprang from her perch.

Aeda walked casually at first to avoid drawing unwanted attention. Positioning herself out of the Historian's view, she accelerated to a brisk pace, gaining speed with each step. Certain her target was unaware, Aeda leaned forward. In a matter of steps she was surging through the crowd, the edges of shirts and sashes grazing her cheek, the market colors blurring like streaks of muddled paint.

Aeda lunged forward and extended her hand, stretching to the belt. It was as though time slowed and the world went grey. The thumping of her heartbeat was the only sound in her ears. She closed the final millimeters to the essence pouches. Aching to reach her target, the tip of Aeda's finger brushing against soft leather. *The reward will be beyond dreams,* echoed Braedyn's voice, the wistful hope this might be the last theft she would ever commit spurring her on.

The grasp of a large, callous hand ripped Aeda back to reality. Her arm locked in place, Aeda's ears filled with the shouts and cries of market-goers. She looked up, and the Historian's stalwart, cold, and imposing gaze greeted her. The Thief attempted to free her arm but for all her flailing and twisting and pulling, her arm would not move even the slightest bit. The Historian grinned and spoke calmly.

"You should know it is not advisable to steal in Biersport. The Grey Society does not view unsanctioned theft in a particularly positive light."

A wave of nausea rushed over Aeda, shocked at her predicament and the Historian's knowledge of the secretive organization.

"I'm surprised the Society has not yet approached you," said the Historian. "Especially at your age, if you have been thieving in the markets. How old are you, fifteen, sixteen? Anyway, I very much think you should reconsider your occupation."

Gieral lifted the girl's arm, smile fading as she reached into her satchel. After furiously rummaging through the bag, Gieral squeezed the Thief's wrist, forcing the girl's hand open. Aeda recoiled and flinched as the Historian thrust a blunt object into her hand. Her shoulders eased at the sight of a plump, ruby-red apple resting in her palm.

"Find something better to do with your life, something more meaningful than taking things that don't belong to you," counseled the Historian.

With that, Gieral released the girl. Aeda paused only for a moment before dashing off into the crowd.

Gieral reached back into her satchel and retrieved a piece of dried and sugared fruit. Her enjoyment of the sweet treat soured at the sight of an odd man at the fringe of the plaza. Conspicuously crouched behind a stall, his gaudy clothes betrayed his attempt to avoid notice. He jumped under the Historian's gaze, standing and throwing his glance to the side. Unsettled, Gieral hurriedly checked her pockets and pouches. Her finger sunk into a gap, tapping an empty brass clasp where an essence pouch should be hanging.

As her eyes darted back to the man, he fled into an alley. Gieral charged through the crowd, market goers parting for the stampeding Historian. A short way into the shadowed alley, she overtook the stumbling man. Stuck in a dead end with his back against a grimy wall, Braedyn stood as proudly as he was able. The Historian drew her sword, its honed edge glimmering.

"I take it you're a Steward for the Grey Society. Rather

bold to be stealing from a Historian, would you not agree?" she quipped.

"What are you talking about?" he stammered.

Gieral thrust her blade between his legs, the tip slamming into the sandy wall, sending bits of crumbled grit and mortar to the ground. Braedyn threw his arms back, letting out a stunted shriek before peering down to see the sword resting between his knees.

"Come now, there's no need to be coy. You had no reason to flee unless you knew what happened and were involved, and I suspect were the orchestrator," she responded cooly. "What were your Thief's instructions? Where is she taking the essences?"

"I don't know what you're talking about," Braedyn spat defiantly. The Historian pulled her blade upwards, the tip groaning unsettlingly as it scraped against the wall, clods of sand breaking against the razor edge. "What… what are you doing?" He exclaimed, his eyes bulging. The Historian glared at him, continuing to raise the blade. "I don't know anything!" Panic rose in his voice as the sword continued to scrape upward, jerking against pits and crags in the wall. Braedyn stood on his toes and gripped the wall with his palms, attempting to delay the arrival of the rising edge. He broke as he felt the cold steel pressing through his trousers.

"She was supposed to bring them to me!"

Gieral stayed her hands, lowering her blade just enough for Braedyn to stand flat on his feet. "And what then? Surely, someone other than a Fence would be destined to take a Historian's essences?

The Steward relaxed and crossed his arms. "How do you

know about Fences?"

The Historian stared at him frigidly, then posed to move the blade again, spurring Braedyn's response.

"Not to a Fence! We were to take them directly to an Attendant."

"Tell your Thief there has been a change of plans. She is to meet the buyer directly, on the centermost pier of the fishing docks, when the third moon is at its peak. Do whatever you need to convince her. If she is not there, I will find you. We will have another chat. And I guarantee it will be less pleasant than this one."

Gieral sheathed her blade with a flourish and exited the alley. Braedyn fell to his knees, trembling.

With her trip disrupted, Gieral made her way to the chambers of the Assembly. Sitting on the divide between the sunny markets of the city and the shrouded Cliff District, the home of the city's government held a commanding view of Biersport. The building was opulent, with marble arches framing colorful frescoes depicting seagoing adventures and topped with pointed green roofs which towered above the city's skyline.

Guards stood in a ring at the steps leading to the chambers, though the empty street made their presence seem wholly unnecessary. Gieral raised her tome, and the sentinels parted way.

Past the antechamber, with its domed ceiling and conspic-uously bare walls, Gieral turned into a modest circular room with no roof. The afternoon sun shone brightly, illuminating a Runetree surrounded by pure white sand. The Runetree was dark and short, its broad trunk angled sharply as if the wind and sea had beaten against it every day. Branches swept back and forth in innumerable tight bends, tipped with pale green leaves. Translucent pink, tan, and yellow runes glowed over the surface, moving in spurts of motion like water striders on a pond.

Gieral knelt before the Runetree and held the spine of her tome in her left hand, retrieving her stylus with her right. The wooden instrument was the size of a pen with a pointed end but no nib or ink, rich brown like freshly tilled earth and covered in intricate carvings. She tapped the end of the stylus on her chest, then on her tome, then pointed to the tree. Her eyes closed, she relaxed her left hand, and the tome levitated; the cover flew open of its own accord and the pages turning back and forth. Specks of blue and white light streamed from her chest to the Runetree where the runes spun rapidly around the branches then surged into the tome.

After a few minutes, the tome shut and dropped to her hand as the runes calmed. Gieral smiled and bowed to the Runetree.

Aeda sat on the edge of a decrepit, abandoned pier in the Cliff District. In her left hand she squeezed the leather pouch of essences, carefully toying with it, while in her right sat the red apple.

When she heard and felt the rhythm of footsteps on the jetty, she tucked the fruit in her satchel. Gripping the pouch, she rose to meet Braedyn.

CHAPTER

THREE

Aeda lay on her mat, beneath the light of a single candle, alone with her thoughts.

Braedyn spoke of us, the two of us, skipping a fence and taking the essences to an Attendant. Now, he asks me to meet a buyer on my own? Who is he to disappear, leaving me as if this were no more than a pouch of coin? And what changed?

Typical.

And yet not typical. She had held the pouch the entire day, the leather unnaturally warm to the touch. Undoing the brass button, she peeked inside. The essence pulsed as if it had its own heart, with blending ribbons of royal purple and ivory white. It was unlike anything Aeda had ever seen before; a thick ooze rooted in the pouch even when held upside down. *It's no wonder it has the power to change fortunes. I've stolen jewelry and gold, letters and wallets, but this essence…* Noticing the candle burning low, she tucked the pouch away and scaled the ladder.

The evening wind carried a biting chill, which sent shivers through Aeda. Overhead, all four moons filled the sky as if they were near enough to touch, the city glimmering as if coated in frost. Aeda paid the view little mind, singularly focused on Braedyn's unusual request. It was unlike her normally self-assured Steward to be nervous, and the sudden change in plans made her wary.

She passed through the Grand Plaza, the previously bustling and energetic space now silent. Merchants had loosely draped cloths over their carts, though goods waited for the morning unsecured. Aeda smirked, knowing the Assembly boasted about safety and the excellent skill of the Biersport guards. In truth, the Grey Society was the real reason such wares could remain comfortably in view, as theft occurred only at their discretion.

Aeda stepped through a passage in the shoulder-height wall that separated the market from the docks and eased down the gently sloping stairway. A lone person stood at the end of a vacant pier.

Aeda walked gingerly, her pants billowing in the wind. With each step, the figure grew larger, though a hooded cloak and the moon behind their back made it impossible to distinguish any features. Aeda approached until she was a few paces away from the unmoving individual. She quivered, filled with trepidation, though she tried to convince herself it was due to the breeze.

Antsy in the uncomfortable pause, Aeda revealed the pouch of essence. The figure thrust out a gloved hand, palm up, expectant. The Thief retracted and brought the essences to her chest.

"What of the payment?" Aeda asked.

"It is rude to sell things that don't belong to you. Besides, you should consider this more to be a return of goods to their rightful owner, rather than a sale."

Impossible. Aeda's heart raced. The Historian drew back her hood and tilted her head with a knowing look.

Aeda turned and dashed away. Gieral charged after, powerful steps pounding the pier like mallets beating on a drum. Aeda's lungs filled with cool night air as she kicked her legs into long strides, running as fast as she could, up from the docks and into the city. The *thump, thump, thump* of the Historian's beating steps continued, ever so close behind her.

Realizing that she could not simply outrun her pursuer, Aeda turned abruptly and broke away from the main avenue. She slipped into a dark alleyway, hoping to stall Gieral. In the scant moonlight of the alley, the Thief and the Historian stumbled through brooms and buckets and laundry hung to dry.

Aeda spared a glance back to see the Historian gaining ground. She looked ahead and the side of an abandoned market stall filled her eyes. She jumped and kicked off the alley wall, landing on top of the cart. Hopping down, she jogged at an easier pace, confident the obstruction would delay the Historian.

A boom cracked through the alley. Aeda turned to see Gieral had run straight through the cart, splinters of brittle wood blasting apart as the tenacious pursuer advanced through the wreckage.

What do I have to do to lose this woman? Aeda fumed. She ran with renewed motivation, bursting out of the alley and onto an avenue. As she hastened up a hill, the Historian blistered behind, nearly within arm's reach. Aeda cut to the left, running atop a retaining wall between tiers of the city. The hard turn did little to slow Gieral, who soon recovered her speed.

Aeda leapt from the wall and landed on the tiled roof of a house. She cautiously danced across the ridge. The Historian jumped immediately behind her, sending clay shingles crashing into the street below. Aeda slipped down a gap between two houses, continuing in the shadow.

Gieral vaulted back to the retaining wall and ran above, bits of rock and sand scattering onto the girl. The Historian dropped down, dirt roiling in a gust. Aeda narrowly evaded Gieral's outstretched hand, slipping out of the alley and into the main street.

As Aeda rushed into the moonlight, she saw two patrolling guards. She latched onto a wooden post to stop her momentum. Guards approached from ahead while the Historian's boots hammered in the alley behind. Options limited, Aeda grabbed hold of the wooden braces and scurried up the tower.

Before Aeda could properly survey her position on the platform, the tower tremored. She hazarded a peek down to see the Historian ascending. Aeda stepped back, shocked to see the Historian's hands gripping the edge of the platform moments later.

Gieral swung herself onto the platform as Aeda jumped to the rim of a channel. The girl danced deftly along the wooden edge towards the next tower, keeping her balance with arms outstretched. Tiring of the chase, Gieral stepped into the channel, forcefully trudging through the knee-high water towards her quarry.

Aeda leapt to the next tower's platform. There was a row of blackened metal levers linked to axles and gears to control the flow between towers. The sound of sloshing water drew her attention to the Historian, who waded through the channel at a startling pace.

Why won't you give up? Aeda seethed as she yanked a lever. A metal gear whirred in the night. The platform slowly lowered, tilting the channel and easing Gieral's approach. Aeda tried to reverse the lever but it would not budge. In a panic, Aeda pulled and pushed the other levers, causing gears and cogs to groan and clink as they spun. A crane arm swung, a rope whizzed on a spindle, but nothing hindered the approaching Historian. Aeda returned to the first lever and shoved it forward with all her might until the metal clunked against a tower post. The platform catapulted up, sending a surge of water at Gieral. Despite her strength, the torrent threw the woman onto her back and carried her away.

Aeda grinned as she slipped down the platform and made her way back to her hovel.

Safely inside the cistern, Aeda glared at the humble surroundings while she contemplated her predicament. *Oh Braedyn, proving yourself to be as wonderful as ever! Was he working with the Historian from the start? Was the Society itself working with her? His excitement about the mark seemed genuine… What does it matter? I can't go back to him, and as useless as that scab is, or was, he was still my connection to the Society. I'm clearly on my own, dealing with this Historian. And what kind of possessed horror is she? I've never seen such a relentless pursuer. What am I to do now?*

Guards had caught Aeda thieving once and the silence of prison had been horrifying, but never had she felt so alone as she did in that moment. *What choice do I have except to stow aboard a ship, to sail away from this Historian, away from the*

Society, away from the Known Lands entirely?

She gathered what few things she had, stuffing little trinkets pilfered from past marks in her satchel beside her remaining provisions. Stepping onto the ladder, she saw the apple on the ground, a smudge of dirt on the otherwise pristine red skin. She leaned down and snatched it, forcing the fruit into her satchel.

As she lifted herself onto the cobbled alley street, she felt someone grab her by the shoulders. In a flash, the hands lifted her into the air and brusquely set her down. Aghast, she turned to see Gieral, still dripping wet. Aeda lunged away but her legs flew out from beneath her and she fell, air punched from her lungs. Her arm dangled above, an iron chain linking her wrist to the Historian's.

"Oh!" Aeda gasped and crawled up to her knees, sitting on her feet. Her heart sank. Head down, she focused on Gieral's damp leather boots.

Gieral released a disappointed sigh as she loomed over the cowering girl. The woman reached inside the Thief's satchel, combing through the menagerie until she stood triumphant with essences in hand. With her pouch returned to its rightful place, Gieral studied the girl.

After a few minutes, the woman finally broke the quiet. Her voice was oddly comforting, like a warm blanket on a chilly day.

"You should have listened to my advice, Aeda. Though I suppose by the time I finished speaking, it was already too late," Gieral chuckled. "Come on then, stand up. You can't sit there forever."

Why is she lighthearted? Hunt me down like a rat on a ship to make light of it all? Aeda wanted nothing more than to burst and let the Historian know her mind, but she refused to give her a scrap of anything.

Gieral offered a hand, but Aeda dragged herself up on her own, like sap pulled from tree bark.

The girl's expression of despair amused Gieral. Aeda stood no taller than the Historian's shoulders, lean with a gaunt olive-toned face and sharp, hawkish features. Sun-lightened hair topped her head. Gieral mused that the girl's hair looked, if possible, even more ragged than she remembered, as if snipped by a blind barber. Aeda's eyes were pale blue-green, the color visible as the sky brightened with the coming of dawn.

"These chains are brutish, aren't they?" Gieral gave them a shake. "What's your name?"

"You already said it," Aeda retorted.

"What is your full name." the Historian's voice cut through the air like a whip.

"Aedreana," she whispered in reply.

"And what is your surname?" Gieral asked kindly.

"I don't have one."

"Well, then Aedreana of Biersport it is. You may call me Gieral."

Unable to resist, Aeda snidely questioned her captor. "And what is your surname?"

She expected an angry response, but Gieral laughed heartily. "I am from the Moor. Unlike Biersport natives, people from the Moor don't typically have surnames. So, as with you, I have just one name, Gieral. If you want to be overly formal, you may refer to me as Gieral of the Moor, mark of the White Crane."

Breaking from conversation, Gieral retrieved her stylus.

Aeda's vision blurred and her temples pulsed. *I shouldn't have expected it to be long before finding out what she's going to do to me.*

Holding the stylus like a quill, Gieral dipped the end into the recovered pouch of life essences. Facing Aeda, she wrote three runes in the air with elegant and crisp motions, the silhouette of each character suspended in place. She swept the tip of the stylus through the middle of the runes in a single, clean motion. The gleaming runes twisted and melded as they gushed forth, a soft lilac glimmer swirling around Aeda before dissipating.

"What… what was that?" Aeda nervously asked. She felt nothing at all, leaving her all the more apprehensive about the purpose of the runes.

"That was a runeword, binding you to me," responded Gieral, unlocking the chains and tossing them aside. "The first rune was for your name, the second, for the binding, and the third, my name."

"What do you mean, a binding? Why are you are binding me to you?"

"It is a way for me to keep you nearby in a more civilized manner than shackling you in irons. Think of it a bit like the chains, but less of a physical attachment and more of a personal connection. Until I relinquish you from this bond, you will feel your very soul pulling you back to me if you attempt to run away." She gazed intensely at Aeda.

Gieral relaxed, then leaned away. "No point in sleeping now. It is nearly morning and you have already packed. Come, we have a long day ahead of us."

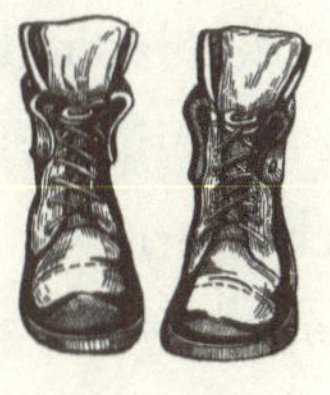

FOUR

Gieral left the alley without further comment. Aeda shouldered her satchel and scurried after, not sure if she was ready to test the binding.

Light crept over the ocean behind them as they meandered up the avenue. Doors creaking open drew Aeda back to the prior morning, as she hopelessly wished she could start that day over. Gieral took long strides up the hill, the outer walls soon filling their view.

"Where are we going?" Aeda hesitantly ventured.

"You stole from me, and infractions against a Historian require a Judgement," Gieral responded over her shoulder. "For this to be carried out properly, we must go to the Great Library in the capital of the Known Lands, Amrodesa."

"But you've got your pouch back," Aeda protested.

"That does not change the fact that you stole it."

Dread washed over Aeda. *What could this Judgement possibly be? It sounds worse than a night in a jail cell, and this Historian speaks as if I should know what she means... to leave Biersport...*

As she shuffled behind Gieral, Aeda spied Jeobinas. The

Steward's face turned from dumbfounded upon seeing the Thief to terror upon seeing the Historian. His reaction fueled Aeda's fears, sending her stomach churning.

I'm used to accepting my lot, resigned to whatever might come. Now, being hauled away by this Historian, somehow it feels… exciting? Amrodesa… I've heard stories, but what will I actually find? What lies beyond the gates I've never left?

Braedyn's shoulders slumped and his legs dangled from the edge of the pier where he met Aeda the day before. His Thief was gone, and his own future unclear. Soft footsteps approached, and he jumped to attention. The Attendant's emotionless eyes seemed to perceive all of his fears in a glance.

"What are you doing?" She said, her words ever-sweet. She continued without allowing Braedyn to stammer a response. "You have work to do. This is not the time to sulk. Finding a Thief as talented as Aeda will be quite the task."

"Am I not expelled?" hesitated Braedyn.

"Of course not. Though you and your Thief may have failed, and I would advise you to never deal behind the Society's back again no matter the risk to your own wellbeing; not a single other Steward attempted to acquire the essences. At least you have your bravado, and for the time, that is enough to entertain the Council. Now, on to finding your next protégé."

The sky brightened to an eggshell blue in the early morning.

After a brief stop by the stable to gather Gieral's mule and horse, they set out. The animals following Gieral without leads intrigued Aeda, but her jaw slacked and she gasped at the expansive fields. *Who knew the world was so big? No walls or alleys, it's as endless as the ocean! Whatever Judgement might await, at least I was able to see this.*

They reached a split in the road at the top of the first hill, Gieral choosing the narrower path. Cool air and warm sun made for pleasant travels. For hours they continued, sand turning to dirt as Biersport disappeared from view. Few travelers went by, none particularly notable save one man riding a donkey and wearing a spiraled blue hat, topped with a bright pink tassel that flopped buoyantly as he wobbled along.

As the day wore on, the steady pace of the Historian after the sleepless night left Aeda drained. The allure of the bright fields of grain had long waned when she cried out to her captor.

"Why have a horse and a mule if you are going to walk?"

"Yes, I think it is a good time for a short rest," replied Gieral.

Irritated at the evasive reply, Aeda plopped in place, a puff of dust curling around her. She pushed aside the red apple and pulled a strip of smoked fish out of her satchel, gnawing on the dry meat. Gieral stepped past Aeda and rummaged through the cart. Exhaling with satisfaction, she tossed a waterskin, a pair of leather shoes, and a thin object wrapped in parchment in front of the girl.

Aeda unwrapped the paper to find a square of bread about the size of her hand inside. It was thin and firm, with slices of vegetables mixed in the batter. She took a timid bite, finding the morsel delightfully sweet. Between mouthfuls of her own loaf, Gieral finally answered the girl's question.

"The horse and mule are companions as much as they are tools. It is important to show them care and respect so that when we have need, they are not only ready to serve, they are eager to. Also, we're in no hurry. Historians are not generally troubled by the comings and goings of the world. Rushing from place to place does little to enhance or expand upon what we see and record. No, I don't think we have need to burden them on such a beautiful day."

Aeda took a swish of water. Upon finishing the bread, she turned to the shoes. They were pale grey and soft to the touch, with firm leather soles and dark blue woven lining. She slipped out of her rope sandals and into the shoes; the cuff rose above her ankle. She closed her eyes and wiggled her toes, the comfort bringing a smile to her face.

She opened her eyes and found Gieral watching. Aeda's grin faded to a scowl. Gieral smirked and resumed their trek.

They marched on through the afternoon, the waist-high fields of wheat fading into short, pale blue-green grass specked with dark brown stones covered in ochre moss. There were twisted trees with coiled branches no taller than Aeda, tipped with long and narrow yellow leaves. Ahead of them, the path sloped gently upwards and the squat stones and trees grew taller and more dense.

Aeda struggled with exhaustion as the world rose around her. The stones stretched higher until they were more than twice as tall as Gieral and as broad as the cart was wide. The loops of tree branches intertwined and reached above the tops of the rocks, so dense that more shadow than sun reached the ground.

Agile birds hunting for insects chirped and flitted between the boughs and boulders.

The change in landscape had been gradual and as the sun waned, Aeda snapped to attention, suddenly realizing how foreign her surroundings were. Ahead was a densely packed forest of trees with smooth trunks and broad leaves. The thick canopy coated the ground in darkness. Tree roots dipped into a tranquil stream with a small wooden bridge spanning it. The gentle gurgle was a distant reminder of tumultuous ocean waves. Gieral unbridled the mule and horse in a lush clearing. Aeda collapsed next to the cart, nestling into tufts of grass.

The quiet was interrupted by a thud near Aeda's leg. She propped herself up and spied a hatchet, its head concealed in a hardened leather sheath. Removing the cover, she discovered a brightly honed edge, though years of use left its cheek scarred.

"Aren't you afraid I'll try to kill you?" Aeda dared.

"Not in the slightest. You're a Thief, not an assassin," replied Gieral, tapping a finger on the hilt of her sword. "Gather some dry wood for a fire while there's still daylight."

Feeling slighted that Gieral showed not even a smidge of concern, Aeda hooked the hatchet to her belt. Seeing little in the way of fallen branches by the grassy clearing, she struggled to her feet. She grumbled as she hobbled on throbbing legs over to the wooden bridge. *I might as well be hungry in the Biersport jail, waiting for Braedyn to get me out. What's better, being in a cell, lonely with an empty stomach, or being a captive dragged across the world?*

The bridge arced gently over the stream, split logs with smooth grey faces lashed together with thin strands of green and yellow rope. Aeda froze as her first step echoed hollowly. Easing forward more carefully, she silently crossed the bridge. Hatchet in hand, she set to her task of breaking and gathering fallen limbs.

Returning with arms full, Aeda found Gieral huddled over a black pot beside a shallow dirt pit, already home to an organized stack of logs stuffed with kindling. Aeda unceremoniously dumped the deadfall, dusting off bits of bark and plopping down. Her brief rest was interrupted by Gieral, who shook a string of waterskins and motioned for Aeda to fill them in the stream.

The water was unexpectedly frigid, swirling into the waterskins. Aeda gritted her teeth and splashed her face, wiping away sweat and dust as shivers ran up her arms in protest.

Back in the camp, Gieral traced a rune in vibrant red essence as smoothly as a swallow in flight. She struck the rune with her stylus and it crawled forward, igniting the carefully laid branches. After the initial surge calmed, Gieral tucked the pot into the fire. Aeda was relieved to finally sit without interruption, bringing her legs to her chest and resting her chin on her knees. Basking in the soothing warmth of the embers, her head drooped.

Aeda jerked awake at the sound of clinking metal. The sky was dark, the moons muted by wispy clouds. Gieral was kneeling in the orange glow of the dwindling fire, portioning out stew. A wonderfully rich aroma of unfamiliar spices reached Aeda, her stomach aching as she accepted a bowl.

Hot food was a rarity for the Thief, her meager income necessitating a diet of dried fish, raw vegetables, and plain bread. In contrast, the thick stew was warm and rich, with peppery spices bursting like firecrackers around hearty chunks of meat and vegetables. Aeda inhaled the contents of the bowl, noisily scraping the bottom with her spoon while Gieral's bowl remained more than half full.

"You can have some more," offered the Historian, turning the ladle towards the girl.

Aeda eagerly filled and consumed a second bowl, and then a third. Stomachs sated, they lay on bedrolls close by the fire, the smoldering embers crackling and spitting as if to sing a lullaby. Snuggled in the plush fur padding and her belly full, Aeda felt an odd sense of comfort and dreams came swiftly.

Gieral inspected Aeda's face, wondering how the girl had become a Thief. Quite tired herself, she set a few larger branches over the coals and pulled her sword to her chest, appreciating the patterns in the stars above before drifting to sleep.

CHAPTER

FIVE

Aeda's eyes snapped open. The four moons shone brightly, casting the world in a hazy white glow. Blinking away sleep, Aeda surveyed the camp. The hot meal had been delicious, yet she did not relish the idea of hard travels leading to an uncertain Judgement. The Historian lay sleeping, hand firm on her sword. *Is the binding that powerful? Gieral started a fire from a runeword, but could one be enough to keep me from leaving? A mere word, more powerful than the will of a person?*

Aeda stealthily slid from her bedroll and slipped into her boots. With the hatchet hooked to her belt and satchel over her shoulder, she crept away. A light wind whistled through the trees and the murmuring of the stream masked her footsteps.

When the last trace of the fire disappeared from view, she broke into a run, legs pumping like a hummingbird's wings. She ran as her lungs dried and cracked in the cool night air; she ran as her legs ached and burned; she ran as her heart beat against her chest like a drum; she ran past the point where she felt she could run no more.

Her feet finally betrayed her as they snagged a tree root. Aeda flew and landed with a thud on her stomach, the last breath fleeing from her lungs. Gasping, she abandoned attempts to rise and collapsed to the forest floor. Her heaving slowly subsided, dizziness lingering. Still wheezing, Aeda gathered her strewn belongings, stuffing shells and rings and other oddities back into her satchel.

As she tucked a brass coated lizard's skull into the bag, a pang came from her palm. She cursed at a thin trickle of blood rolling down to her arm like dew on a blade of grass. Aeda crawled to the stream, dunking in her hand. She recoiled from the stinging cut, though the water was curiously warm.

The bright red apple sat invitingly at the top of her satchel. Aeda scrubbed its skin and took a bite of the sweet fruit. As she ate, she listened to the soothing song of water batting against rocks. Ripples in the creek shimmered. Aeda looked at her reflection, her tattered hair pointing every which way. An odd calm washed over her as she peered into the mirror image, and the urge to take a sip overcame her. She leaned in when a light whisper came, seemingly from everywhere at once.

"Don't go."

The hair on Aeda's neck bristled. She scanned the surrounding forest, between trees and across the stream, seeking the source of the words.

"Please don't go." The voice came again, hollow and thin like the echo inside a shell.

Aeda leapt to her feet. *Is this the binding?* The apple dropped from her hand. The voice chilled her, goosebumps creeping across her skin like a swarm of ants. She shrunk, folding her hands across her arms as she sought the source. In the unknown dark of the woods, she felt a painful longing to be back in her warm bedroll at the camp.

Aeda gasped as the voice rang out again, this time closer, its words filled with desperation. "Don't leave me!"

"Who are you?" she yelled back. "Where are you?"

Her words echoed in the trees, followed by a thunderous silence. Aeda received her answer when the stream bubbled, drops of water popping as they landed on the shore. The stream ceased flowing and instead oscillated and churned, twisting and swaying rhythmically. The water rose in a spout, splashing as the swell formed the shape of a child.

As the bubbling subsided, the stream surged up into the apparition, then trickled back down. Aeda's curiosity drove her to take a few tentative steps into the creek bed. She fell back as two holes appeared in the suspended flow, in the space where eyes should be had it been Human and not water. The figure fixated on her. It spoke with a voice that boomed with the intensity of stormy ocean waves crashing against the shore.

"Do not go," it commanded.

Terror filled Aeda as she looked through the face of the apparition. In its presence, the desire to return to Gieral rose. She achingly hobbled along the bank back the way she had come, watching the pulsing and undulating figure during every step.

She had expected the swell to dissipate, but it moved upstream alongside her. Wondering if it was guiding her back, Aeda halted. The apparition paused, water continuing to flow through its form. *Could a runeword conjure such a being?* Aeda cautiously approached until the tip of her shoe pushed a stone into the creek, and the figure tensed.

"YOU WILL NOT GO" it roared. The outline burst into an enormous, rapidly spinning waterspout. Foam sputtered as it brewed and broiled, and spurts of steaming water sizzled through the air. Aeda mustered what little energy she had and bolted. Fearful of being lost among the trees, she hazarded a path next to the creek, hunching low as streams of water hissed by.

Without a backward glance, she fled until the bridge came into view, her pace dwindling to little more than a casual stroll. The disturbance in the water had subsided, not a ripple in the creek to show for the figure's presence. Aeda sighed in relief as she stumbled to the camp on legs as sturdy as strands of damp hay. She shivered away a chill as she slipped into her fur bedroll by the still flickering fire, pleased to see Gieral unmoved.

A thud on Aeda's heel startled her, and she pulled her knees to her chest. Wrenching her eyelids apart, she found Gieral hovering above. The sun was rising, casting rays of golden light across the tops of trees.

"Good morning, I trust you slept well?" inquired the Historian. "Little can compare with a good night's rest in the woods by a tranquil stream with a warm fire. It is past the time to rise. Once you eat, we will be on our way."

Aeda resented the cheery tone and thoughts of sleep, but the prospect of food was enough to alert her. She sprang up, regretfully sore and teetering unsteadily.

All signs of their stay had vanished, save her bedroll and the little black pot, open with a spoon in it. *How did she clean the entire camp without waking me? Ugh, my back. I can't believe I slept on my satchel. I never even took my boots off.*

A bowlful of stew, delicious even when cold, tempered Aeda's mood. Gieral instructed her to clean the pot while she cleared the scant remains of the camp. Aeda recoiled at the chilly bite of the water when she dunked the vessel into the stream.

"The water can be quite cool," called Gieral. "Perhaps not as warm as you might have been expecting."

"It was cold yesterday," Aeda meekly replied, turning her hand to hide the tender scrape. *She must know I left in the night, that I tried to break the binding, seeing as her runes conjured the boiling creature in the stream.*

"Ah yes, of course. I was thinking of the ocean you are familiar with, being quite warm throughout the year."

Aeda shook the pot dry, relieved that Gieral's response bore no mention of the figure in the stream. Spying a particularly smooth stone in the streambed, Aeda slipped it into her satchel. She scurried after and tossed the dish into the cart, taking a position between the horse and Gieral as they crossed the bridge.

Entering the woods, the sun disappeared like a torch doused in water. The understory was open; the view filled with wavy branches crawling up to a dense canopy where scattered flecks of light between leaves glimmered like seashells on a distant beach. The uncannily flat leaf-covered floor was dull and colorless beneath Aeda's feet, longing for the sun to find its way down.

They marched onward and Aeda soon grew weary of the forest. Eventually Gieral stopped, taking in her surroundings. Aeda dismissively slouched against the cart. *It all looks the same. Now, a few minutes ago, a few hours ago, what's the difference?*

It might as well be days. Everything is the same, the same trees everywhere.

Gieral tossed a piece of candied fruit to the girl and munched on her own.

"This forest is rather boring, isn't it? There is a quaint town in the heart of the woods. Unfortunately, it is a bit out of our way." Gieral turned to Aeda. "I'm sure your fatigue is just in your mind. You will feel refreshed once we're back to open fields. It might not look like it, but we're taking a substantial shortcut and we will be out soon enough. Navigating a forest like this one isn't quite as simple as following a stream."

Aeda's ears burned, though Gieral paid her little attention. The horse and mule followed Gieral as she stepped off the road and into the forest, the cart bumping against Aeda's shoulder. She rubbed her arm, biting into the candy to curb her desire to protest. Aeda's cheeks could not resist puckering into a smile from the sweet treat.

Joy from the candied fruit waned as travel off the path slowed to a sluggish crawl. *Shortcut,* she scoffed, feeling as though the entire concept of time had vanished. With her interest in the woods long faded, she kept her eyes on her feet to better traverse branches, roots, and rocks covering the forest floor. Marching in the endless gloom, Aeda nearly walked into the cart when it came to an abrupt stop.

Peering around the side, she finally saw the sky between the tree trunks. Rolling hills covered waist-high, deep blue and green grass filled her view, punctuated by stems tipped with pink and grey tufts. A gentle gust flushed through the vale, the meadow soothingly rustling as a small flurry of seeds floated into the sky, glowing bright orange in the light of the setting sun.

Gieral stood and admired the view. Aeda rushed past, stretching out her arms and diving into the field. She spun as she fell, landing softly on her back in a cloud-like cushion of lush grass. Gieral turned to the cart and pulled out two large pasties, stuffed until they might burst from the gentlest of squeezes, and tossed one to Aeda. She took a bite and the buttery, flaky crust crumbled, exposing sweet meats and chunks of vegetables inside. After a few bites, Aeda looked up from the pie with curiosity.

"Why do you have so much food? And how do you keep it all from spoiling? I don't think any of this is from Biersport."

"As to why I have so much food, I often travel for a long time between towns and I enjoy having options," replied Gieral, leaning against the cart. "As to how it keeps from spoiling, we have to expand on our previous discussion of runewriting. Runewriting is useful for many things besides creating a binding or lighting a fire. In most cities, runewriters offer their services to prolong the life of perishable goods for departing merchants. Biersport is unique because of the prohibition of runewriting inside the city, but nevertheless it is still runewriters, outside the walls, who preserve all the fish taken elsewhere in the Known Lands. Once you finish eating, gather some wood for the fire and we will rest."

Aeda voraciously consumed the pasty, licking the crumbs from her fingers. With few words, she and Gieral prepared their camp a stone's throw from the edge of the forest. A cool breeze and sounds of swaying grass lulled the Thief and the Historian to sleep.

CHAPTER

SIX

Aeda rested peacefully, her mind flying among clouds. A distant voice whispered her name. She ignored the call at first. It sounded again, more urgently. Aeda tried to brush it aside, but the call came a third time, cracking through her dream like a whip.

"What," she hissed.

"Aeda," whispered Gieral. The Historian spoke coldly, her face blurred in the dark. "Don't move, and be quiet. When I tell you, run into the woods as fast as you are able, then hide. Hide and do nothing else. Do you understand?"

"Yes," whispered Aeda, puzzled by what prompted the order.

Gieral closed her eyes and clenched her fists tightly around the grip of her sword, the leather groaning and creaking. Her hands stilled on the blade and a painful quiet settled over the camp. Aeda shivered with unease. *She's genuinely fearful. What could such an immensely powerful woman, a Historian, be afraid of?* Then, through the subtle chatter of grass in the breeze, she heard a familiar sound. Muffled footsteps approached, carefully measured to avoid detection.

Fear welled in Aeda as the intruders neared, blood pounding louder in her ears with each hushed step. Her legs twitched, aching to run. Cold sweat beaded on her brow when the sound of footsteps ceased by the edge of their camp, replaced by the rustling of hands taking hold of swords. Aeda could hardly bear waiting any longer when Gieral's eyes opened. She nodded to Aeda and rose.

"Run!" she yelled, the word breaking the still of the night. Aeda scurried to her knees but froze at the sight of three dimly lit figures. Brown masks covered their faces, hoods pulled low. Snug leather jerkins extended down below knees, with arms and legs wrapped in woven strips of leather which blended into their gloves and boots. Brandishing swords, they braced as Gieral lunged like a wolf after deer.

The Historian raised her blade, deftly dropping the tip to her side before bringing it across the nearest foe. The assailant deflected the strike, but the force threw them onto their back. Turning to the unmoved girl, Gieral roared again. "Run!"

Aeda sprang to her feet, slipping around the cart and scampering to the forest. Behind her, the piercing clash of metal rang. Aeda ducked down behind a large root just inside the woods and turned to watch.

Gieral wielded her sword with great speed. Her strikes pulsed like a metronome, each twist, each turn, each swing of the blade a brutal yet perfectly rehearsed motion. The brigands fought in concert, drawing out to one direction as another would flank from the opposite side, but Gieral rebuked every assault.

Steel clanged as Gieral brought her blade down on a bandit's sword, forcing them to their knees. She swiftly kicked the second, knocking them to the side, then slashed up and across the third. Aeda gasped as red flecks floated through the sky, painting the Historian's sword crimson. The brigand collapsed, writhing on the ground, their compatriots fearfully pulling them away by the shoulders.

Gieral leveled her sword and menacingly stared down the assailants. The fight had transfixed Aeda, but a nearby glint of light caught her attention. Between the trees, she saw the outline of a person tracing a bright red and orange runeword that billowed like a roaring fire, hovering between them and Gieral. Focused on the brigands, Gieral was completely unaware of the runewriter's presence.

As the runewriter raised their arm to strike the runes, Aeda took her hatchet and hurled it with every ounce of her might. The hatchet sailed through the air, twisting and turning, tip over hilt, side over side. She grimaced at the hatchet's ungainly flight, yet it flew true to its target and struck the runewriter's arm as their stylus touched the runeword.

The hatchet's edge glimmered red. The runewriter shrieked and the visage of a flaming wolf sailed high above Gieral and dissipated into the dark of the night. Gieral's attention turned to the runewriter, who clutched their arm and fled. With their compatriot routed, the two unharmed attackers broke ground, dragging their wounded companion into the forest.

Gieral stood casually at the edge of the campfire, scrubbing her sword with a rag. Aeda emerged from the woods, approaching with her hand outstretched.

"What did you find?" Asked the Historian, sheathing her sword. Aeda uncurled her fingers, revealing the runewriter's stylus. Smiling thinly, Gieral took the slender instrument and inspected its blackened surface. "Thank you. In part for the stylus, but most importantly, for saving my life."

"Oh," Aeda exhaled, digging at a pebble with her toe.

"People usually say 'you're welcome' when someone thanks them. Or perhaps you regret keeping me alive?" Gieral jested.

"You're welcome," replied Aeda, her voice cracking as she looked at the red-stained blade of the hatchet. *We were nearly killed, and she jokes as if nothing happened. Why did I even throw the hatchet? Why save my captor? And why is she showing me such kindness if the only reason we're together is to bring me to my Judgement?*

Gieral took the hatchet and wiped it down. "It is fortunate this ended without injury to us or death for any of them."

"Why wouldn't you want to kill them? It seemed like they were trying to kill you."

"Death is an unpleasant thing and taking a life can leave a heavy burden. It is easy to speak of taking a life, but to actually take one is an entirely different matter. Have you been around the dead before?"

"Once," responded Aeda, sitting by the fire. "A mark died, right in the middle of his dinner while I was watching. He keeled over and rolled out of his chair, mouth still full of fish. I was waiting for him to be drunk enough to steal a jeweled ring from his finger. The other Thieves were going to wait until he was buried and then dig up his body, but I went into the catacombs first. He seemed oddly peaceful there, laying on the cold stone like it was a feather bed."

"Unfortunately, death is not always polite. I somehow doubt our guests tonight were interested in allowing us to pass so serenely," said Gieral, handing back the cleaned hatchet.

"Who were they?"

"I'm not sure. This path is rarely taken, and common bandits usually stay by throughways where opportunities to plunder are plentiful. Considering their unfamiliar dress and the accompanying runewriter, I expect they were far more than opportunistic highwaymen. It all makes little sense. I have also never seen marks quite like the ones on this stylus. Though I do know of someone who might," she said, tucking the stylus into her belt. "We had better continue on our way. I doubt sleep would come if we were to lie down now."

What has this Historian dragged me into? Aeda was irritable to have yet another night interrupted. *Braedyn may have been useless, but he never caused me to worry about dying. All my troubles in Biersport seem small now. She is right, though; how could I sleep?*

Gieral leaned over the low burning fire and traced an azure runeword with her stylus. Striking it, the blue runes rushed forth and curled into the coals. As if doused with a bucket of water, the embers spat and hissed and smoked. They packed the remnants of the camp, ribbons of orange unfurling in the sky as they finished.

"You asked when we might ride instead of walk? Now is one of those times," said Gieral, mounting her horse and motioning for Aeda to climb onto the cart.

She clambered up, gratefully stretching out her legs as she sat on the padded leather seat. Aeda almost fell off the cart when the mule started after Gieral. Bouncing up and down, she slid to the side of the bench, clutching onto the rails.

The sun crested the horizon as they reached a main road, an inviting avenue of smooth, tawny rocks packed with cracked dirt. Gieral increased their pace to a steady trot, bits of dust flicking up behind the hooves of the horse and mule.

The days that followed blurred together like paint smeared on a canvas. Each day they woke at dawn, pausing only to take out food which they ate on the go, and not stopping until sunset to sleep. Polite salutations to the occasional passerby did little to break the monotony of their constant travel. The sea of tall grass shortened and faded to a mustard yellow, the bright tufts giving way to clusters of lush green trees with drooping branches and rectangular, pale grey stones speckling the rolling hills.

The morning of the third day, they came upon a curious sight. A gaggle of nine Dokkaebi came bobbing down the road, each riding a donkey. The Dokkaebi themselves were lanky, none broader than Aeda, their skin pale in shades of yellow and tan and brown. They had long arms and narrow fingers with thick, squared nails. Angled-back faces hosted large eyes above small round noses and pointed teeth. Atop their heads were wild, curly, and flamboyant hairdos, intentionally worked into chaotic arrangements. Each wore clothes so different from the others that they could not possibly have selected more distinct outfits of color, even had they dressed together with that intent.

Aeda had seen the occasional Dokkaebi in Biersport, but she had never seen a creature like the one following the party. She was awe-struck by the hulking beast, which towered at least eight feet tall with stout shoulders topped by a bulbous oak-barrel of a head. It thunderously stomped on legs as thick as tree trunks. Creases streaked across its leathery, slate grey skin. Chunky, four-fingered hands pulled thick ropes tied to a wagon that held a black metal cube, the vessel nearly twice the size of Gieral's cart. To add to the spectacle, the behemoth armor of dimpled steel plates trimmed in bronze.

Counter to the imposing beast's calm demeanor, the Dokkaebi were in a heated argument, spitting and cackling and yelling amongst themselves. They took a break from their squabble and politely waved and smiled and bowed to the Historian, bickering anew when their salutations were complete. Gieral leaned back to Aeda upon seeing her wonderment at the lumbering beast. "It's an Ogre."

They progressed without incident after the encounter with the Dokkaebi caravan. The morning of the fourth day since the attack was agreeable enough, but by the early afternoon, dark, purple-tinted clouds filled the sky and an unwelcome rain rolled in. Unlike the harsh thunderstorms which frequently battered Biersport, it was a dreary shower.

Gieral pulled her cloak over her head, retrieving a similar one for Aeda. The Historian covered the cart with an oiled leather tarp while Aeda swung on the pale grey cloak. She was delighted as beads of water bounced off the covering as freely as pebbles dropped on rock.

Preoccupied by the dancing raindrops, Aeda hardly noticed as the horse and mule scaled a winding path up a steep hill. Gieral pulled the reins to halt at the crest, the abrupt stop drawing Aeda's attention to the landscape before them.

From their perch, the rolling hills faded into a valley where countless streams intermingled, feeding an expansive, twisting river. Where many of the larger tributaries came together, gigantic outcroppings of rock rose like pillars holding clouds. Aeda guessed they must have been at least as wide as the largest ships were long, and many times taller than the overhanging cliffs of Biersport. She could just make out the thatched roofs of a humble village nestled at the base of the giant columns.

Gieral turned to Aeda, a trickle of rain dripping from the front of her hood. "Welcome to Hrold's Hand."

CHAPTER

SEVEN

As they descended to the town, the verdant grasses receded into patches of prickly, twisted butter-yellow reeds with translucent green edges and sprawling, stubbly vines. Short trees dug in the soggy ground, with crawling roots that coiled over themselves. Their branches spread wide with curled red- and orange-tipped leaves, which turned up to the sky. The monoliths of Hrold's Hand loomed ever taller as they approached. Aeda usually appreciated feeling small and out of sight, but in the shadows of the rock monoliths, she felt positively insignificant. The behemoths towered overhead, with red-and-orange-leaved trees clinging to the rock faces amid dangling moss. Enormous white cranes with long tails and short necks flew in and out from crags and on ledges in the face.

Aeda spied dozens of narrow fishing skiffs made of reeds propelled by long poles across the waterways. A candle lantern with a tin cap dangled from a curved reed at the front of each vessel. The fishers, using every imaginable implement from nets to spears, huddled under giant woven reed covers which looped over their heads around their shoulders, extending past their knees to protect from rain and sun. The path led to a wide reed bridge which sat low over the water, allowing passage over the swirling mud by the riverbank. Gieral hopped down from her horse at the crossing. Aeda climbed off the cart, venturing a question.

"Why aren't there any walls or guards?"

"Despite its impressive appearance, Hrold's Hand is a simple fishing village," replied Gieral. "In times of peace, such as this, walls seem a luxury and most villages lack the wealth to build those like Biersport's."

Instead of paved roads, the bridge led to a lattice of reed platforms which sprawled between homes and stores, elevated above the soppy mud. Every step clinked, and the village murmured like an orchestra of pan flutes preparing for a performance. Aeda shivered at the eerie, hollow echoes in the sullen town.

Mud-walled buildings, capped with reed roofs, jutted out from the monoliths over streams and rivers. Residents wore simple loose pants cuffed at their knees, relaxed shirts hemmed at elbows, and sandals made from strands of crushed and softened reeds. They all donned reed hats with colored strands and unique patterns layered in the weave. Outside each door was a row of hooks to hang hats before entering.

In the dim early evening, villagers placed lit candles in windows and ignited lanterns throughout the village. After stabling the horse and mule, Gieral happily entered an inn carved into the side of a monolith to escape the rain. Aeda paused at the threshold, timidly peering in.

"Come in," invited the innkeeper, a thin man with frizzled

cinnamon hair. His shirt was bright green with a brown apron over top, covered in smears of food and drink. Leaning on a counter, he motioned to the girl. "Come, come, you shouldn't stray from your mother."

The inn was warm and pleasantly dry. Aeda inspected the innkeeper, his face bearing a sweet naivety, the kind of pleasant and unsuspecting person who made for the easiest of theft.

"Oh, she's not my mother," Aeda replied.

"What?"

"She's a Thief," answered Gieral, sorting out a row of five copper nails and taking a key from the distracted innkeeper's open palm. "And my quarry."

"Thank you for the invitation," Aeda coyly added.

"What… what do you mean, Thief? Madam Historian? Excuse me!" stuttered the innkeeper.

Gieral slid a nail of silver into the palm of the flustered man. "Don't fret, she won't be any trouble. We have had a long day on the road. I would appreciate it if our meal is ready as quickly as you are able."

Gieral stepped away down a narrow hall. Aeda tarried, one hand tracing the edge of the counter with her eyes locked on the innkeeper's. A wide, closed-mouth grin spread across her face. The innkeeper snapped his palm shut around the coins, pulling away as her hand passed by. Aeda raised her eyebrows with glee, expression fading as she skipped after Gieral.

The inn had looked small from the outside, Aeda now realizing it extended deep inside the monolith. Layers of flattened reeds dressed the walls and thin cloth hung over the ceiling, but the floor was cold, bare rock. A mild dampness peculiarly reminded Aeda of Biersport.

Gieral had been waiting by the door to their room and motioned her in. "Stores, inns, and many homes are cut into the fingers of Hrold's Hand. There are even some hidden passageways."

Their room was a homely space. Two chairs flanked a square table with an uneven wood top. Two beds sat opposite the table, with a small chest between them. Trails of cooled wax ran down candles throughout the room.

Gieral tossed her bags onto a bed and then excused herself to retrieve their meal. When the sound of footsteps faded down the hall, Aeda pilfered a squat candle and tucked it into her satchel. Satisfied with her acquisition, she plopped into a cushioned chair, swinging her feet as she waited.

Seconds burned into minutes, and Aeda tired of the dull room. Her attention turned to the bags lying on the bed, curiosity growing as to what might be inside. Finally reaching the edge of her patience, Aeda leapt from the seat, popping her head into the hall to look for the Historian. She listened to the muffled menagerie of voices from around the corner as villagers came in for supper, but none resembled that of Gieral.

Back in the room, Aeda studied the bags. She memorized their placement, then carefully unbuttoned the top of the first. Gently lifting the leather, she peered inside. To her disappointment, the bag contained nothing more than a few garments and a roll of bread. Aeda peeked back into the hall, then hastily opened the other bag, which proved similarly mundane. With her intrigue sullied, she arranged the bags precisely as they were before. She sank back in the chair and lay her head down over crossed arms on the table. *I might as well be back in that endless forest. Waiting here feels more like sitting in a jail cell than resting at an inn. Urgh, anything would be better than just sitting here!*

An enticing fragrance alerted Aeda that someone must be coming down the hall. Her nostrils flared and her stomach grumbled deeply for what seemed an eternity. Gieral arrived with a reed platter. Two clay bowls brimmed with a creamy white broth, the ends of roughly chopped vegetables poking out. Two ceramic plates each held an array of three slender fish; one rolled in batter and fried, one blackened and flame charred, and one salted and dried. They lay on a bed of fluffy greens, which were coated in luscious oils.

"Go ahead, you look ready to eat the plate itself," said Gieral.

Requiring no further invitation, Aeda dug in. She passed over the salted fish and plowed through the charred fish, the smoky sweet flesh an enjoyable departure from briny coastal fish. Tangy bits of batter crackled and crunched as she bit through the fried fish, punctuating her bites with spoonfuls of the hearty vegetable soup. When the plates were clear of everything except bones, Aeda's eyelids drooped, weighed down by her full belly and the many days of travel.

"You should rest. We have a few hours until our meeting," said Gieral.

Aeda felt an urge to ask if it was about the stylus, but dazed from the meal, she abandoned her questions and rolled herself into bed. Aeda found the mattress, stuffed with pounded and softened reeds, strangely reminiscent of her straw mat in the Biersport cistern. In moments, sleep shrouded her mind.

Aeda woke to a hand on her shoulder. Gasping, she lurched away, calmly exhaling on seeing Gieral's face. A single lit candle left the room ominously dark.

Aeda blinked away her short-lived sleep, her voice raspy and dry. "What's with you always going out in the middle of the night?"

"I thought you might enjoy another late-night stroll by the water," retorted Gieral. "Are you telling me now that you didn't enjoy our midnight tour of Biersport? Anyhow, it is time to go. You will want your cloak."

The hair on Aeda's neck prickled at the thought of her flight by the stream, easing at the mention of Biersport. Gieral moved wordlessly through the inn. The commons smelled of stale beer and fish, laced with a sweet smokiness from cooling coals. Many guests slumped over tables, asleep, including the innkeeper. A few still nursed their now-warm ales as they muttered hushed conversations in the glow of low-burning candles.

Aeda pulled her cloak in tightly as a rush of cool air greeted her outside the inn. To her surprise skiffs were still out on the rivers, illuminated by their lanterns. One nearby fisher thrust his spear into the water, retrieving a wriggling eel.

Thin wisps of clouds striped the sky, dulling the moonlight. Sour from lack of sleep and the cold, Aeda made no effort to quiet her steps and thumped loudly on the reeds. Gieral abruptly stopped by one of the monoliths. A crevice was barely visible in the meager flickers of lanterns. They shuffled through the uncomfortably tight passage into a reed-walled room.

Three gruff men, each with a bright sunflower yellow sash hanging from their belt, sat around a wooden table. A game on the table absorbed their attention. The centerpiece, a rack with twisting metal arms, had small hooks spaced along its appendages. Hanging from the hooks were cloudy, colored stones caged with wire. Each of the men had a stack of one color of stones in front of them beside a handful of coins, bets placed for their game.

The men rose, looking amongst themselves before facing Gieral. She tossed a small pouch onto the table, all three of the men reaching to snatch it. The first to grab the bag opened it, dumping a few nails of silver and bronze on the table. The man snorted and nodded towards a doorway behind his shoulder.

Aeda stayed close behind Gieral as she ascended a broadly sweeping spiral staircase. The seemingly endless steps grew wider and shallower as they rose. Around the last bend, a raucous din echoed. Gieral paused and locked eyes with Aeda.

"We are about to see a tempestuous man. He will undoubtedly be rude and will probably try to anger you. Ignore him and do not speak a word. Not a word. Let me talk, and hopefully we will be away shortly."

Aeda wanted to question the directive, but Gieral swiftly climbed the last few steps. *Not so different from Braedyn, ordering me around with no explanation.* The passage opened into an expansive gallery with high arched ceilings and bright torch lights all around. Long counters flanked each side of the room, where bartenders served drinks to the unruly crowd. At tables throughout, there were more of the colored stone games crowded by patrons with yellow sashes. Fat pipes belched clouds of smoke which lazed about the room, the sweet yet sooty smell of burnt herbs filling the air. In one corner a lively troupe performed, singers with tambourines jingling and lutists strumming and flautists playing their reeds.

The boisterous party was silenced when the Thief and the Historian entered. Gieral nonchalantly stepped in, confident thumps from her boots resonating through the room. Aeda followed in Gieral's shadow, her shoulders hunching as she shied from the incessant stares. A man broke out into a guttural laughter that pounded through the air like a beaten drum.

Aeda leaned around the side of Gieral and spotted the source, a barrel-chested man clad in layers of tan leather trimmed in golden yellow. His head was shaved, though he sported a thick, dark brown beard. Scars marred his face and his icy grey eyes leered coldly, contrary to his outward humor. He continued to guffaw and leaned back in his chair; the wood creaked beneath him.

Gieral stoically strode towards the man. She was unwavering in her path, bumping into onlookers who stood in her way. Aeda grew increasingly uncomfortable in the wake of angry patrons, one spilling their ale, another slipping and nearly falling. Once she stood directly before the man, Gieral pushed the table with the heel of her boot until it nearly touched his chest. With ample room to sit, she lowered herself to the chair. Aeda, left awkwardly standing, clasped her hands and inched behind Gieral's shoulder.

The man's laughter ceased, and his lip curled into a disdainful expression.

"Welcome, Gieral."

CHAPTER

EIGHT

"**L**ooks like you have a new pet on your shoulder there, Gier. Is it a bird? Or maybe a rat?" The man leaned his head forward with each sentence, tilting from one side to the other.

Aeda's ears reddened at his derisive comments, but she heeded Gieral's words. The Historian crossed her arms. "Go ahead, Jakro. You don't need to pretend you don't know what she is."

"But how did you manage to get yourself a Thief?" he asked, fixated on Aeda as he leaned back into his seat. "The Council doesn't tend to let their little minions stray from the nest, at least not the Thieves or Stewards."

"You don't get to know everything," Gieral intoned.

"But it seems I do know something you don't. What do you have that needs Identifying? You didn't come here to chat with an old friend."

Gieral set the dark stylus on the table just within Jakro's reach. As the man extended a burly, hairy hand for it, Gieral pulled the table away with her foot. Jakro continued to lean, but Gieral kept sliding the stylus ahead of his grasping fingers.

Enraged, the man slammed his fist, the table creaking and splintering in protest.

"Who do you think I am? I am Jakro the Identifier! You come, I look, you pay, simple as can be. If you want to play games, go talk to a tree, Historian."

"Two fingers of gold," said Gieral calmly, as if on the edge of boredom.

Two fingers of gold? The sum seemed ludicrous to Aeda no matter how important this Identifying was.

"What do you mean, two?" Jakro replied coolly. "I thought I said no games, Gier."

"You are not the only Identifier."

"I'm the best you know and I'm the one that's here, six fingers of gold."

Six! Aeda's mind drifted, imagining the treasures she could buy with such a sum.

"Two fingers and one nail of gold."

"You're testing my patience, and we both know there isn't much to test. No more games. Four fingers or we're done here."

"But I only brought three." The Historian's words oozed with obviously feigned innocence.

"I tell you what, I've always wanted a Thief of my own. Leave the girl and keep your gold. I'll take a look."

Hair on Aeda's neck bristled. *Is my worth four fingers of gold? She can't possibly consider his offer! I might be her captive, and it has been far from the most pleasant journey, but I can't imagine living under Jakro's roof to be anything but a nightmare.*

The Identifier grinned. He set his fingertips on the table, forming a cage around the stylus. Gieral kicked the edge of the table, slamming Jakro in the gut and knocking him back. Gieral pulled open a pouch and tossed a finger of gold on the table, the shiny metal rod landing dully as Jakro grumbled. Again, she tossed a finger of gold, clinking against the first. A third joined the pair, Jakro broodingly awaiting the fourth. The corners of his mouth dropped to a scowl as Gieral tossed a nail of gold into the pile, a smirk on her face.

"What did I tell you about games, Gier?" He growled.

She tossed another nail on to the table, and then a third. Jakro took the stylus and settled into his seat, expecting the fourth and final nail of gold to be forthcoming. He placed the point of the stylus on the table, a finger on the other end, and spun the stylus. Gieral dropped three fingers and three nails of silver on the pile, one nail of silver short of the sum he had demanded.

"You're lucky I like you," Jakro conceded, scooping up the stylus. Turning it slowly, he peered over his nose, eyes manically poring back and forth. Aeda shifted to scratch an itch on her leg.

"Stop shuffling, you little dimwit, I need to concentrate. How could you possibly steal anything with the way you stomp about like a drunk stumbling in the night?" Jakro directed his words to the room. Murmurs of agreement and snide laughter came in response. "It was a mistake to bring a fly into a room of birds, Gier."

Gieral was unmoved, though Aeda's cheeks flushed, and she struggled to hold her tongue. She reminded herself of the Historian's caution and checked her temper, not wanting to tempt fate and risk being left with the Identifier.

Jakro guffawed and picked up a circlet from beside the table.

The base was an inch wide band of brass, the inner surface lined with ruffles of black silk. Thin metal arms with lenses extended every which way from the outside. Jakro settled the device on his head like a royal crown, giving the audience a knowing look as the hall hushed.

Jakro dipped his own stylus in an essence pouch, then tapped the side of the circlet. A dull blue haze surrounded the gears as the arms twisted and rotated. Cylinders and lenses of clear topaz snapped down. His eyes magnified to enormous scale through the glass while runes pulsed like a halo around his head.

As Jakro pored over the surface of the stylus, the lenses flipped and spun, changing in and out of his view without guidance. The spectacle engrossed every person in the room; ash in pipes cooled and instruments sat idle. The cycling lenses were the only sound in the otherwise absolute silence. After inspecting the stylus end to end countless times, Jakro leaned back. He lifted the circlet from his face, and the light faded and runes dissipated. Staring at Gieral, he nodded toward Aeda.

"What's a Thief doing out and about with a Historian? What purpose do you have keeping that little toothpick at your side?" He turned his attention to Aeda. "And you? Young for a Thief, aren't you? Didn't make the cut, booted from the Society, was it? I can't imagine how you survived in Biersport. You have got to be the loudest, most irritatingly obvious Thief I've ever seen. Namuor knows why Gier's got you in tow."

"But I haven't said…" Aeda protested when Gieral hissed.

Jakro continued his tirade, giddy at the effect of his words. "A Thief should know better than to speak in the presence of their betters. I should charge extra for having to put up with you, you moron."

The crowd cackled, echoing Jakro's childishly derisive sentiment. As the girl's hands balled into frustrated fists, Gieral's voice cut into the chatter.

"So, Jakro, what is it then?" she asked.

"It's a stylus," he chuckled impishly, the onlookers laughing boisterously.

"And who's playing games now?" challenged Gieral.

Jakro set the tip of the stylus onto the table, one finger on the end of the handle, spinning it with his thumb.

"I don't play games, Gier. And I haven't liked your tone today. Seeing as you shorted on payment already, maybe you should just leave this meager imitation of a Thief here for compensation."

"What did you see?" Gieral commanded, her tone marking the end of the discussion.

"Well, other than being a stylus, I can tell you it's not from the Known Lands. Doesn't seem to be from the Wyrm Adherents either, nor the Desert Dwellers to the north, nor from across the Western Ocean. In short, I don't know where it's from or who it might have belonged to," he said, flicking the stylus across the table.

Without looking, Gieral caught the stylus before it hit Aeda's face. Anger swelled in the young Thief like storm waves in the ocean.

"You don't know? You sit there and question my skills as a Thief? You've never seen me steal, yet you proved that you can't Identify! And you still sit there smug as can be, insulting me!" Aeda erupted, spewing words like water from a pot boiling over. "How sad are you to take payment and then fail to deliver? If

I failed to retrieve a mark and went to a Fence, do you think he'd pay me for my empty hands? You are nothing more than a tiny fish in a giant sea, wishing you were a whale, drowning in your own inability. You don't know?!"

I've gone too far. Aeda realized the foolishness of her outburst, clasping her hands. Jakro leaned on the table, the wood groaning beneath his balled fists as he menacingly rose like an enraged bear.

"Thank you, Jakro. We will take our leave," interjected Gieral.

The Historian hoisted Aeda under one arm and took long strides to the exit, the girl's feet all but dangling in the air. Behind them the Identifier roared, spitting insults and curses until his face turned blue, the crowd too stunned to act. The casual strength of the Historian took Aeda aback, and she nearly fell when released at the stairway.

Without a word, Gieral hastened down, her pace difficult for Aeda to match. The Historian brushed by the three men in the antechamber and went straight to the exit. The guards, too distracted by Gieral marching by, failed to notice Aeda swipe a blue stone from the table.

They sped through the village and back to their room in silence. Gieral eased the door shut and spoke before Aeda could ask what Jakro had meant by Namuor.

"I told you not to say a word," said the Historian, her voice wavering. "That may not have been what you expected, but that does not mean you should speak out. Jakro excluded the entirety of the Known Lands and its neighbors as the origin of the stylus. It was well worth the price. And besides, people don't go about calling themselves Identifiers without cause. It takes decades of travel and study to build the skill and knowledge necessary to take on that mantle. Despite his demeanor, as insufferable as he may be, Jakro should have had your respect from the start. Respect is something that should be given freely and may only be lost, not the opposite, as many believe."

Aeda was sore at the admonishment. "He lost my respect by doubting my ability when he couldn't Identify anything about the stylus."

"I thought we already covered your misconception about his ability," cut Gieral. "While he might toss insults like a farmer sowing seeds, Jakro is not one to take them lightly when directed his way. He is all but the king of Hrold's Hand and with him in such a mood, we won't be welcome for long."

CHAPTER

NINE

A dragonfly bumped into Aeda's arm, pulling her from a daze. The prior night, Gieral had left the horse and mule with a courier and purchased a river barge. Aeda was wary at first, the boat tiny and unstable compared to the seafaring ships docked in Biersport. Worse still was the haunting wind which seemed to carry whispers of Jakro's bellows, chasing them from Hrold's Hand.

By the morning Aeda found the rocking relaxing as she looked out from the bow, though she still felt the sting of Gieral's admonishment. She was irritable about the entire episode. Aeda tried to suppress the part of her that was upset because it recognized her own part in their hasty departure.

The river gently meandered, a steady flow with placid ripples on the surface. Tall red grasses and taupe trees with emerald-green leaves clung to the banks, their long branches reaching over the water. To the right, densely forested mountains covered the distant horizon, snow-capped stony crags cutting through trees at the peaks. To the left, mustard and tan fields expanded as far as Aeda could see, peppered with tiny domed purple flowers hanging from curling ferns like miniature grapes from vines.

They spent two quiet days on the river, passing the occasional fishing boat and cluster of houses. In Biersport, the tense anticipation of her next assignment clouded her scant idle time. Now, Aeda found herself enjoying the quiet interlude, her thoughts of the coastal city fading like drawings in the sand with the coming of the tide. In their place were feelings of freedom and an enjoyment of traveling, tempered by trepidation over what the Judgement might entail. She tried to push aside thoughts of the impending event, passing time making bracelets from seashells and watching for people on the shore.

On the morning of the third day, the world appeared to end on the horizon. Aeda saw nothing except the sky visible above the river. Bare rock burst through the ground, forming walls on either side, framing clouds like a picture. Aeda covered her ears as the gentle lapping of ripples rose to a booming rumble. Before the end of the river, she saw a tangled web of ropes hanging low, lashed between hooks anchored in the rock.

Aeda was relieved when Gieral directed the barge towards a small village tucked away on the left bank. Stone buildings with mud and thatch roofs crowded around a long, sturdy pier which sloped out into the river like a hand ready to catch passersby. Gieral rose as they neared the jetty where two men were standing. They wore oil-slicked pants and snug leather coats, their heads topped with short, pointed hats with curly fur trim. Tufted flaps hung from the hats, shielding their ears from the din.

Aeda was studying their hats when the men each grabbed a rope from the pier and jumped high into the air, hovering for a moment, then crashing onto the barge in unison. She clambered back as the boat shook, sending wakes across the river. The men crossed their arms and held the ropes over their shoulders, the boat arcing around the jetty as the river pulled against their grasp.

The men's faces broke into smiles when Gieral held out two silver nails. *I could have stolen her coin instead of the essence and had my world changed. How did she acquire such wealth?*

Payment in hand, the men looped the ropes through the barge's railing and leapt back on the dock, one helping Gieral and Aeda up a ladder while the other secured the boat to the pier. Aeda nearly jumped off the edge of the dock when rough hands pulled a hat snugly over her head without warning. The two men doubled over in what Aeda thought was excessive laughter, though she swiftly became grateful for the fur flaps which doused the thundering of the river to a soothing rustle.

Aeda and Gieral slung their bags over their shoulders and proceeded down the jetty. A few villagers ran out from their stone dwellings and hurried past them. Aeda watched in fascination as they pulled the barge along the pier and raised it up onto the rocky shore. Once on the ground, they began dismantling the craft with oddly shaped tools.

Gieral led away from the busy villagers and across the town. Buildings had exceedingly thick stone walls, the hefty construction necessary to dampen the constant bellow of the river. At the outskirts, Gieral took off her hat. Aeda followed suit but regretted her choice, finding the river still uncomfortably loud.

"How can they live like that?" Aeda roared, but her voice

was barely audible.

"Yes, they are quite nice, are they not?" Yelled Gieral.

Aeda was flustered, which she believed could as easily have been a misunderstanding as an intentional deflection. Resigned to follow, she threw her hands in the air and set after Gieral. They descended a stone path out from the village, the trail cutting into a narrow passage with mossy rock walls on each side. When the noise subsided to a low rumble, Aeda called out again.

"How can those people live there? And why did you pay them if they are just going to tear the boat to pieces?"

"They live in Crost because, for most, it is the only life they have ever known. People grow accustomed to their unique ways of living, so it is difficult to leave. That is why Bog Elves tend to live in the Bog and Dokkaebi in Ulburis. Not because they dislike other places, rather they are comfortable with the lifestyle they were raised in and find it difficult to change. Regarding the barge, it was part of our payment. They keep us from falling off the edge, and in return, we pay a small sum and they keep the vessel."

"Falling off the edge of what? And if the boat was payment, why did they take it apart? Why pay them as well?" Followed Aeda, still incredulous.

"You will see the 'what' momentarily. As for why they took it apart, once they have disassembled a boat, they take the parts to other villages upstream. There, they reassemble the boat and sell it. You may feel the price is high, but Crost is far and away the most expedient way to Amrodesa. The high cost is for our time, which is one of the most valuable resources of all."

They scrambled a short way further and rounded a corner

and the walls receded, opening the world before them. The trail descended into a vale rippled with rivers glowing in the late morning sun. The heart of the basin was home to an impossibly tall forest of trees with ashy brown mottled trunks and a lush canopy. Winding through the outer edge of the forest was a tan and grey wall, with buildings clustered along the perimeter. Caravans and travelers, specks in the distance, were coming and going on roads radiating out from the city.

Looking away from the city and to her right, Aeda finally saw what Gieral meant by the edge: a rocky precipice where the river fed an enormous waterfall. A torrent spewed out, then dropped hundreds of feet and crashed into a giant pool below. *For the expansiveness of the ocean, for all the rain in the storms, I never imagined water could be this beautiful.*

"We should be in Amrodesa by evening," said Gieral.

Navigating down a series of switchbacks and steep declines consumed the rest of the morning. Houses and mills dotted the valley, with farms and pastures increasingly covering the land as they neared the city. Water wheels fed raised wooden irrigation troughs, the channels a distant reminder of the towers in Biersport.

The sun hung low as they approached the outskirts of Amrodesa, afternoon rays bursting through the canopy. The trees were even taller than they seemed from afar, soaring into the sky, their leaves shades of indigo and olive with flashes of yellow streaks.

Buildings in Amrodesa were almost all three stories tall. Tan and grey stones packed with a sandy mortar formed the first floor walls, atop which sat the second and third floors of wood painted in pale almond and milky white shades. Aeda marveled at the plentiful windows filled with large panes of glass. Maroon tile roofs topped the buildings. The homes and shops and storehouses were interspersed between trees, cobblestone roads weaving through the forest.

A gaggle of children ran across the road, some swinging sticks like mighty swords, while others kicked and chased a painted leather ball. Aeda was especially curious about a Spriggan child who, instead of hair, had stubby horns which looked like tree branches atop her head. A hammer clanging on glowing metal drew Aeda's attention. Blacksmiths with stained brown aprons and hulking leather gloves tended their smithy, the forge illuminated by vibrant flame.

The path rounded a corner, and an open gate came into view. White banners emblazoned with a yellow sun and surrounded by blue and green leaves flanked the entrance, hanging from beams at the top of the walls and nearly touching the ground. Guards leaned on long spears with white flower-like tassels hanging from the heads. They wore shimmering steel scale armor beneath white tabards bearing the same yellow sun, with tan boots and gloves. One nodded and smiled cheerfully at Aeda, who found herself quite uncertain how to react.

While Amrodesa hosted a multitude of guests from all across the known lands, the local fashion was quite opposite to that of a Biersport native, and Aeda felt out of place. Residents wore colorful patterned vests over loose shirts and slender pants woven with dark thread. Aeda turned her attention from the clothing to the face of a Sea Nymph, admiring her ethereal, teal-toned skin, high cheekbones and ears which looked like delicate silk fans. Gieral addressed Aeda, who had been staring unintentionally rudely.

"It must be different for you, seeing so many races and in such numbers. Thanks to the Assembly's xenophobia, Biersport is rather inhospitable if you are not a Human. While not every city is as diverse as Amrodesa, most are at least willing to open their doors for people of all races. If a Sea Nymph merchant sought entry to Biersport, they would likely never be called by the guards."

"Do people here not care about race?"

"There are some cultural tendencies to consider, but that's more to be courteous than anything else. Aside from that, most don't care in the slightest. And why should they? Does it not matter more how a person acts as opposed to how they look or where they're from? Not everyone from Biersport should be treated as a Thief."

Inside, the city was bustling. Aeda found the enormous trees, some as wide across as houses, even more impressive than the monoliths of Hrold's Hand. A short way past the gate was a sprawling market. The lack of stalls and carts intrigued Aeda, each store housed in its own building in a ring around the plaza. Stands and displays protruded through open windows and sat on tables outside to entice customers, while large painted signs with colorful art and calligraphy drew the attention from afar.

Aeda drank in the sights, spying a store with only scrolls and no books, its neighbor having only books and no scrolls. Next was a bakery with long skinny loafs of bread, followed by a garden shop with a green and yellow awning covering mountains of seeds and pots with pretty flowers. Across the street, a butcher chopped and carved hunks of meat for customers, and on the other side of a massive tree, a grocer displayed pristine fresh vegetables as crisp as if just pulled from the ground.

Adding to the splendor of the city were countless performers. It seemed that every corner was home to a busker, some juggling swords and torches and spitting fire, while others sang and played instruments exquisitely, inviting onlookers to gather and dance.

Gieral slowed by a hill topped with a tranquil grove of squat trees, no gaps in the branches which bent to the ground. Separated from the rest of the city, Aeda heard few sounds aside from birds chirping and leaves rustling in the gentle breeze.

They passed through an archway into a grassy knoll with large tree roots rippling through the surface. Before them was a mammoth building made of square-cut white stones with swirls of lavender, red, and grey. The building had three sets of wide stairs leading to a veranda on the main floor. Tall columns supported a roof of burgundy fish-scale tiles. Aeda was stunned, the elegance starkly different from any building she had ever seen.

Gieral paused and offered an introduction. "Welcome to the Great Library, home of the Librarians, sanctuary for Historians, and catalogue of all the history of the Known Lands."

Aeda followed the Historian up the steps. *Why am I wishing this journey wasn't ending? I can tell myself I'm fearful of the Judgement, but there's something else… Free from the Grey Society, gone from Biersport, never a missed meal… The adventures on the road, I've never felt this excited and free. I could never have imagined all the things I've seen, places I've been. If it hadn't been for Gieral, I'd still be sitting on a pier in Biersport, dreading the moment Braedyn would bring a new mark. If only we had a few more days…*

As they reached the veranda, a boy ran out of the library. He wore a dark blue tabard emblazoned with a silver branch in the center; beneath it was the simple clothing typical of all Librarians: tan pants, a loose white shirt, and thin, light grey boots. He placed a hand on his belt, which held essence pouches, and bowed deeply. Gieral returned the gesture as the boy, no older than Aeda, brushed his unkempt hair from his face. He slung their bags onto his back and scurried into the library.

A Librarian came, his tabard bearing a tree encircled by leaves, and embraced Gieral warmly.

CHAPTER

TEN

The atrium was a humble space with no furnishings aside from a few simple benches. The stone walls felt cold in their emptiness. In contrast, huge wooden doors hung open in the entryway, bound in metal trim and engraved with coiling branches, roots, and leaves. Directly across from the doors was an exceptionally long hallway, nearly as wide as a city street. Aeda spied the edge of a giant tree in a room at the end of the corridor. A few young boys and girls with blue tabards gathered nearby, listening to an older woman speak. Smaller passages branched off to each side of the atrium, illuminated by orbs of warm orange light hovering by the ceiling.

Gieral and Aeda followed the Librarian down one of the side halls. They passed countless open doorways, some arched, some square, some pointed, some with fancy carved trim while others had no trim at all. As varied as the doorways, the rooms ranged from cozy to voluminous and came in every imaginable shape. The one consistent feature was a Runetree in the center of each. The Runetrees were more varied than Aeda believed possible, home to runes in a myriad of colors pulsing and dancing along their surfaces. Librarians attended to guests in many of the rooms, while in others they knelt before the Runetrees in quiet meditation.

The trio entered a spacious oval room with a Runetree whose trunk was thin enough for Aeda to wrap her arms around, its straight branches growing up through the open ceiling. The Runetree's bark was pale lilac-grey with arrow-shaped mossy green and brown leaves, the runes on its surface flickering pale blue like ocean waves at dawn.

A shelf encircled the room, stacked with scrolls and books. Stones paved the perimeter, but yellow grass covered most of the floor. The stiff blades appeared sharp as knives, yet under each step, the tips curled and the grass softened like velvet, springing up again when the intruding foot was raised.

From around the Runetree a portly man shuffled into view, his wispy hair and beard bouncing with each step. His clothing matched the other Librarians except for an ornate tabard crested with a Runetree, flanked by two smaller Runetrees and encircled with two rings of leaves. Hands behind his back, he alternately tucked his upper lip beneath his lower lip and then his lower lip beneath his upper lip. He grinned, the Historian bowing in reply.

"Gieral, my girl, glad to see you. I didn't think you would be back so soon." Despite his jittery mannerisms, the man's voice was reassuring. He clasped his hands, flicking his thumbs back and forth as he spoke, a tinge of uncertainty creeping into his words as he eyed Aeda. "Who… what brings you back?"

"Head Librarian, thank you for your gracious welcome. We need to prepare for a Judgement." Aeda stiffened at Gieral's emotionless words.

"Well," he replied, voice cracking. Fidgeting with an imaginary loose thread on his tabard, he stalled for an uncomfortable minute, then dropped his hands and clapped them to his sides. "I will make the arrangements. I suppose it is a bit late for today. We will start in the morning. Ferin, you can be the reader. Off you are then. We will reconvene tomorrow."

He forced a sheepish grin, then tottered out. Ferin bowed and exited; Aeda assumed to prepare for whatever her Judgement might entail.

Gieral led further into the Library, turning into a secluded room. It was home to a toffee-colored tree with ribbons of burnt orange streaking its trunk. Cloudy grey leaves with ruby veins covered its drooping branches. Sunflower yellow runes faded in and out of view. The last rays of early evening sun illuminated the soft green moss with red tipped tendrils that covered the ground.

"Do you know what the purpose of Runetrees is?" Gieral asked.

"No. No one ever said much about them." Aeda circled the Runetree, mesmerized by the runes which shimmered and glistened like dew-covered flowers at dawn. *They're beautiful. No gem or jewelry I've ever seen could compare.*

"Of course, keeping a stranglehold on information is a Biersport Assembly specialty. I may as well tell you while we have a moment. As you have seen, Runetrees fill the Great Library, each with its own room. These Runetrees store all of history. Not as simple facts or events as written in a book, but with emotions, feelings, the heart of truth. All the details which we are too feeble to remember, all the sensations that are impossible to capture with words, are encapsulated and stored here. The runes carry bits and pieces of history, bound to the Runetree like letters printed in a book, except they are imbued with life."

"But how do the runes get there? Braedyn said nothing of Runetrees, only that Historians record history in their tomes. You don't write in them?"

"We do record history in our tomes, but not by writing."

A woman entered the room, dressed in the now-familiar garb of the Librarians. She shared a polite bow with the Historian and nodded to Aeda. Gieral unlinked the chain to her tome and handed it to the Librarian.

She knelt in front of the tree, holding the tome upright by the spine at shoulder height. The pages remained shut even as her fingers released their grip. She wrote a single pale blue rune above the tome, then delicately guided her stylus through it.

The book levitated a few inches above her hand and the cover peeled apart until it was flat, as if resting on an invisible table. The Librarian wrote a long series of intricate blue runes, then struck them. A bright gold glow emanated from the pages and they flipped as if caught in a tornado, seeming to go both forward and backward simultaneously. Runes poured forth in a torrent between the tome and the Runetree. The bark glimmered and the runes pulsed erratically, as if bustling aside to make room for new runes to join.

The furor and brightness eased, and Gieral continued. "Historians commune with Runetrees across the Known Lands to record history in our tomes, and in the process we transfer our own experiences to the volumes as well. Historians are, however, prohibited from transcribing to Runetrees. Our friends and compatriots, the Librarians, take care of that responsibility. They, in turn, are prohibited from recording in tomes. When we return to the Great Library, Librarians transfer the regional history from our tomes to Runetrees. This is the basis of our partnership as chroniclers and stewards, neither complete without the other."

"What about people who aren't Historians or Librarians?" asked Aeda. *What about people like me?*

"Everyone has an absolute right to access the recordings. The people you saw in the other chambers likely came to the Great Library to learn about some past events with the assistance of the Librarians. Some might even wish to contribute their own memories, which the Librarians can also help with."

"They looked like normal people," remarked Aeda, questioning whether commoners were important enough to have their lives recorded.

"Anyone who wishes to share their thoughts is welcome to do so. Every person, whether a wealthy royal living in a fancy manor or a pauper from the streets, has value. In recording history, we should never consider a life inconsequential, as we all are important in our own way. No two people have the same perspective, therefore the more people who contribute their experiences and memories, the more complete our recordings become."

"You said there's a Runetree in Biersport. How many are there?" Asked Aeda, wondering why Gieral was sharing openly on the eve of her Judgement.

"Come with me, the transcription will occupy the Librarian for some time yet and we should not disturb her work." Gieral walked leisurely into the hall. "Aside from the Runetrees housed in the Great Library, there are many more spread throughout the Known Lands. In the heart of the Great Library is Namuor, the first Runetree and home to all history. At the eve of time, nine branches were cut from Namuor and planted to establish the nine cities of the Known Lands. From the nine trees, more branches were taken and planted in towns and villages throughout the region. Most of the major localities have a Librarian or some other officiant who tends their Runetree, and likewise, each city has its own rules surrounding them. Unfortunately, in Biersport, none except for Historians are granted access to the Runetree."

"If people aren't allowed to visit, how is history recorded?"

"A Runetree is much more than a book or a plant. Through the earth, the air, and the water, Runetrees are ingrained in their locale in ways beyond our understanding. Imagine a beach, full of pearly white sand. That is what the Runetree will capture on its own, the background of a painting, if you will. What people add through their memories are the shells, crabs, the birds in the air, the sounds of the water splashing, the scent of sweet, salty air, the little details that bring the story to life." Gieral stopped at a hall lined with four arched red double-doors. "Ah, we're here. These rooms are for visiting Historians, we can leave our belongings and clean up before dinner. I'm sure you're hungry."

"I'm staying with you?"

"Yes, why would you not?"

"I'm not a Historian and the Judgement is tomorrow," Aeda said in a hushed voice. *It's usually the nicest exteriors that hide the worst inside. The Great Library is magnificent. I dare not imagine what awaits.*

"You have not yet been judged, so you're in my charge for now. No one will treat you differently than any other guest until the Judgement is complete."

A simple but cozy room waited behind the doors. It was as if a mirror was in the center of the room, with beds, chairs, small tables with water basins and candles, and chests of drawers all placed symmetrically. Carved out of a cranberry-brown wood, the legs and trim appeared like trees, with handles shaped like leaves. Gieral set down her essence pouches and satchels, then took off her pauldrons, vambraces, greaves, sword, and cloak before untying her hair.

She had been stoic and intimidating on the road. With all the layers removed and her hair falling over her shoulder in tangled waves, Aeda found her almost fragile, like a normal person she might pass in a market with no particular notice. Gieral washed her face in a basin and Aeda followed suit, scrubbing grit and grime away from her face and arms with warm water, patting dry with a plush grey towel adorned in sky blue stitching.

Refreshed, they made their way further into the Great Library. Aeda's nostrils flared as they passed through a stone arch, and the sensational aroma of a masterful kitchen greeted her. She heard voices in bright and cheerful conversation, growing louder as they entered an expansive dining hall. Librarians of all ages mingled at wooden tables and chairs filling the moss-floored room. The ceiling was open to the canopy of broad leaves. Aeda's stomach grumbled loudly as she sat with Gieral.

A Librarian appeared with a laden platter, while another brought them plates, knives, and cups filled with sweet berry wine. On each plate were two folded towels, one warm and wet, the other crisp and dry. The utensils were little more than a distraction to Aeda as she ogled the platter. There were slices of hard cheeses, mounds of milk curds, dollops of jams and mustards and jellied sauces of bright colors, slices of glazed fruits and fleshy nuts, hunks of breads both fluffy and flat, braised meat falling apart under its own weight, and an assortment of charred vegetables glistening in seasoned oils. Aeda's eyes swelled. Gieral spoke as the girl reached for the spread.

"Dinner in Amrodesa is typically served on a platter like the one before us, though the Great Library is admittedly a cut above the norm." The Historian's voice froze Aeda, her hand hovering over a piece of tender meat, face coated in disdain. Gieral continued casually. "Use the knife with your right hand. Your left is for grasping food. The wet towel is to wipe away crumbs, the dry towel is to wipe away oils and sauce."

Aeda slowly took the knife in her right hand, setting her left on the edge of the table. She paused in anticipation of further instruction. Gieral instead reached over to the lump of roast meat Aeda was previously reaching for and sliced off a large portion. "I thought you were hungry. What are you waiting for?"

Aeda required no further invitation and furiously tore into the platter. Gieral sat back, eating at a measured pace. After Aeda had tried a significant portion of everything, she eased to a more reasonable rate of consumption and Gieral spoke again.

"I'm sure you must have more questions. Now would be the time to ask them. That is, if you can manage to find space in your mouth to form words."

Aeda gulped back a piece of fruit, still leery. "Why are there so many rooms with Runetrees? Why not have all the trees in one room, or record everything on the first Runetree?"

"There is a separate room and Runetree in the Great Library for each of the original thirty Historians." Gieral replied. "We bring our tomes to the same Runetree as our mentor, and the Librarians complete the transcription. Afterwards, the most senior and skilled of the Librarians will commune with the Runetrees in these rooms and then commune with Namuor.

"Thus, one tree does contain everything. But if you were to commune with Namuor, it would be a different experience than communing with one of the other Runetrees, even if you were to relive the same event. The perspective and heritage carried on through each Runetree is unique and something to appreciate on its own. Think back to Biersport. The day and night I spent there would be drastically different from your view compared to mine. If we combine the events from both of our views, then a more holistic view would emerge. However, some of the individuality would be missed. Having the separate Runetrees allows us to keep that bit of personality without marring the truth."

"When you commune with a Runetree, are you recording everything that has ever happened wherever the Runetree is?"

"While that might be possible, to do so would require sitting for many, many hours, perhaps even days. Beyond not having the patience for it, we would record a great deal that is already known. Instead, when Historians commune, we record from the present and go back until we find a time when another Historian was there. We tend to go a little past that point to be sure our recording is complete, but this way we keep our records complete without spending hours communing. The Librarians appreciate this as well, as it takes much longer to transfer to Runetrees than it does to record from one."

Aeda chewed thoughtfully and looked through the open roof at the leaves rustling overhead, the sky darkening between the leaves. "How did you become a Historian?"

"I grew up on the Moor, far to the east. It is a cold and barren place, unlike Amrodesa or Biersport. One day, when I was not much younger than you, a Historian arrived wearing only one shoe. I overheard him mention that in his travels, he had lost the other shoe when fleeing a pack of wolves. Being foolish, I went out on my own and found his boot, though I discovered the wolves which had pursued him. Upon successfully fleeing, I returned his errant shoe. The Historian invited me to join him on his travels, and I accepted."

"What about other Historians?"

"For many Historians, becoming an Apprentice was a matter of happenstance. Although our purpose is clear and defined, Historians as a group are loosely organized. For the most part, there are more liberties than rules. For example, there is a well-defined process for officially declaring an Apprentice, much like the procedure for a Judgement. Yet when it comes to the selection of an Apprentice, we are essentially unrestricted."

"I see."

Aeda's response was meek and sullen. *Why answer my questions? Why tell me anything at all with the Judgement tomorrow? Does she have some further, yet-announced plans for me?*

The two finished their meal quietly and retired to their room.

Gieral slumbered easily, but Aeda stared at a flickering candle. She found a strange sense of longing for Biersport, for her hovel under the streets and the freedom to come and go as she pleased. With the Judgement weighing ominously, sleep was a distant dream.

Retracing her steps from the afternoon, she returned to the room with the tan and gold Runetree, lying on her back beneath its branches on springy moss. Gazing at the night sky between the leaves, she tried to predict what the morning might bring.

CHAPTER

ELEVEN

Aeda woke to footsteps faintly tapping down the hall. A young Librarian, no more than a year or two apart from her in age, trotted in boisterously. The girl's face was rosy, with prominent dimples framed by silky black hair. She smiled widely while Aeda scrambled up to her elbows.

"I'm Iyra, I suppose you're Aeda. Gieral said you need to clean up. Sorry, that sounds rude. Those were Gieral's words, not mine! I'll show you the baths so you can have a proper wash; there's an area especially for Historians. I think you and Gieral are the only ones in today. It should be all yours." The Librarian's voice was light and kind. Iyra offered her hand, which Aeda cautiously took.

"I heard there will be a Judgement today," Iyra said, turning away from the Historians' chambers.

"How did you hear about m… the Judgement?" Asked Aeda. "Are you going to be there?"

"There are only a few hundred of us Librarians, so news travels quickly. Judgements aren't an open invitation affair, though. I doubt many people will be there. I am curious about what it will be like; I've only been able to read about them. Do you know what the Judgement is about?"

"I'm not certain," Aeda lied, leaning hoping to catch the Librarian's expression. *Is she playing coy? She seems too friendly, and she never did say if she would be there or not.*

Iyra turned into a round room of grey slab stone filled with the sound of flowing water. There were a few chambers, each one shielded by a wall of dark grey stone. Iyra motioned to an alcove where a stream of water poured down from the ceiling.

"Gieral had clothes sent for you. They're inside this one. Maybe I'll see you again later," Iyra said with a parting bow.

She definitely knows more than she's letting on. Brushing aside thoughts of the quizzical Librarian, Aeda ducked behind the stone curtain and quickly disrobed. Stepping under the shower, she relished the warm water. Inside a pleasant cloud of billowing steam, she scrubbed with a pumice stone. *This is probably a special preparation for the Judgement.* The thought sullied her contentment. She stood a few moments longer, almost wishing she could put back on the layer of grime and return to the road.

Aeda dragged herself out and patted dry, looking at the clothing set aside for her. She pulled on trim tan woven pants and a simple sleeveless white muslin shirt that extended a few inches past the waist of the trousers. The material was comfortable, though the pants felt foreign compared to her customary billowy pants.

Aeda gave her head a hefty shake to dry her hair, her seashell bracelets and anklets clinking. Her leather boots sat caked in muck. Aeda walked out barefoot, dirty clothes and boots in hand.

She hustled nervously back towards the Historian quarters.

Passing Librarians bowed to her in greeting and Aeda found herself awkwardly bowing in response, unsure if she was leaning far enough or bending too quickly. *Blasted customs, this is why I prefer alleys.*

Back in the chambers, she found Gieral bent over a shirt, brow furrowed, a needle in hand. "You should eat some breakfast. Unfortunately, morning meals are not so grand as supper in Amrodesa."

Gieral's relaxed demeanor left Aeda more uncomfortable than before, as if there were an itch on her back that could not be scratched. Shivering away the pestering sensation, she sat in front of a wooden bowl full of sliced fruits surrounded by a pool of thick white cream with toasted black bread. She spooned up a mouthful and grinned with delight.

The needle between Gieral's tough and leathery fingers looked like a strand of seaweed on a mile of beach. She wielded it like a sword with motions that were neither delicate nor fluid, punching systematically as if she were battling the thumb-sized hole in a shirt. It was comedic to Aeda; the needlework seeming more effortful for Gieral than driving away bandits in the night.

Her humor was short-lived as Gieral tightened down a knot, tossed the shirt to the bed, and tucked the needle into a spool of thread. "It's time."

Aeda forced down a final morsel of bread. She wiped her sullen face and followed Gieral. The curls in Gieral's hair twisted and flowed in waves behind her, Aeda keeping close in her wake. With each pulse of Gieral's harshly thudding boots, the beating of Aeda's heart rose, banging and pounding against her chest, begging for her to flee. The tormented walk felt agonizingly long, as if they were walking the distance back to Biersport.

They arrived at the chamber in the heart of the Great Library. For a moment, Aeda's fear subsided, and she stood in awe of Namuor. The Runetree was enormous, its trunk as wide as a river, spearing up from a bed of curly moss into the sky so high she could not tell where it ended. The bark was colored in ribbons of cloudy greys and chestnut browns, mottled and specked with hints of sage green moss. Innumerable pearly alabaster runes surged across the Runetree's surface, the color more pure than the brightest of whitecaps on waves. The ends of the broad and flat leaves, in shades of jade and cobalt blue with flashes of yellow and lilac veins, curled down to fine points.

Aeda barely noticed the rest of the room, the space circled by white columns, a small arched recess with a bench between each. The Head Librarian arrived with Ferin, bringing Aeda's mind crashing down from the peak of the Runetree. Gieral bowed to the Librarians, Aeda imitating the gesture.

"Well, I had better explain what a Judgement is to the girl." The Head Librarian grumbled and squished his chin down, eyeing Gieral. He shifted his focus to Aeda, eyebrows raising on seeing her bare feet. He sighed solemnly. "Simply put, a Judgement is a… review of a person and their actions. Rather than having a Historian give a potentially biased account, we have a Librarian read from the Historian's tome and abbreviate recordings of the person being judged. Ferin will do that for us today. He will provide his recounting openly, that you will know we are not unjust in our review. Once we have examined the past, the Historian provides their recommendation, and it is my responsibility as Head Librarian to apply a final Judgement."

Aeda stood awkwardly under the Head Librarian's gaze, her face scrunching into a grimace. Realizing the Head Librarian was waiting on her, she stammered a response. "I understand."

"Right, and what is your full name?" He asked.

"Aedreana."

"Aedreana what."

"Just Aedre…"

Before she finished her name, the Head Librarian flapped an outstretched hand, motioning for Ferin to begin. The Librarian carefully wrote a blue runeword over Gieral's tome and struck it with his stylus. Instead of a flurry of runes flowing forward, the book cracked open and rose a few inches, a gentle flow of runes lazily coursing between the flipping pages and the Runetree. A pale silver glow settled over Ferin, and he breathed deeply.

"Gieral traveled to Biersport, concerned for Kinoh, a Historian whom she had not heard from for much longer than she expected. After arriving, Gieral caught a girl in what she believed was the attempted theft of her coin purse. Given the girl's bedraggled appearance, Gieral presumed the girl to be an urchin and warned her of the danger of stealing for those not a part of the Grey Society. She gave the would-be thief a piece of fruit and released her into the crowd. Moments later Gieral spied a Steward. She discovered her pouch of life essences had been stolen. Her first thought was that the unkemptness had been a clever cover for the Thief."

"I thought we were talking about actions, not fashion…" Aeda murmured under her breath. The Head Librarian shushed her with a hiss and a whistle. *How is it fair to be judged but not be allowed to express my opinion?*

"Gieral found and spoke with the girl's Steward, confirming Aeda was indeed a Thief of the Grey Society. They arranged a meeting for Gieral to recover the stolen essence. She hoped the girl would return the stolen goods, but when confronted, Aeda ran. Gieral gave chase through the city and into the night. After tracking her down, she cast a runeword to remove the binding of the Grey Society. She stated the runeword was binding Aeda to her and they would travel to Amrodesa for Judgement."

The Head Librarian rippled with irritation. "Why would you do that, Gieral? Why did you have to abduct a Thief? And then lie to her?"

"What do you mean, the Grey Society's binding?" Followed Aeda.

Gieral motioned for Ferin to proceed. "They traveled without rest until the evening. Aeda ran away during the night, which Gieral allowed, viewing it as a test to see if the flight would weigh on her conscience. Pleased with her appearance back at the camp, they traveled for another day. That evening, a group of unknown assailants appeared. Instructed to flee, Aeda ran to the edge of the woods, assisting Gieral by interrupting an unseen runewriter. Aeda found the stylus of the runewriter and traveled onward for four days, barely pausing until they arrived at Hrold's Hand."

Flustered, the Head Librarian again interrupted. "Gieral, all I am noticing is your deceit. I have to remind myself this is the girl's Judgement and not yours. And don't tell me you took her to see Jakro. Gieral!"

The Head Librarian is a curious man, more worried about Jakro than the fact that we were attacked? And of course, Gieral knew! All those jabs, speaking of walks in the night and streams, she was making light of me all the time.

"They took a short rest in an inn, then proceeded to the gallery, where Gieral brought the runewriter's stylus to Jakro. He knew nothing of its origin and the Thief challenged his competency. With Jakro enraged, they quickly left, the Thief pilfering a game piece during their exit." Aeda flushed bright red. "Gieral led them out in the night, purchasing a barge from a merchant. It took three days on the river to reach Crost, and shortly thereafter, they arrived in Amrodesa."

The tome shut, and the rune-glow faded from Ferin. The story vexed the Head Librarian. He ran a pudgy thumb in circles against the outline of his index finger. "You steal a Thief from the Grey Society, let her run wild in the night when she has certainly never been out of that city before, nearly get her killed by highwaymen, then introduce her to Jakro. Maybe it should be you standing for a Judgement and not her. What is your assessment then, Gieral? Hm? How judge you this girl now you have fully ripped her away from her life and nearly killed her in the process of bringing her here?"

What life was I taken from? A life of servitude to a society which barely acknowledged my existence? I was a ghost in the streets of Biersport, yet here is this stranger and she was aware of every step I took but said nothing at all. What will she say now?

Gieral replied in a measured tone. "They were not highwaymen, but we can discuss that later. When I first saw Aeda, I was not sure what to think. Better to end the interaction and move on with my duties. Instead, she interrupted my travels in ways I did not think possible.

"She stole from me without my realization, which is embarrassing yet also impressive. She then proved her persistence with the ridiculous chase, later finding her conscience when she remained, despite having ample opportunity to leave. She likely saved my life by interrupting the runewriter despite it being against her own interest, and although inappropriate, having the gall to make her voice well known to Jakro showed boldness and a desire for fairness. Through it all, she has shown a refreshing curiosity."

"And your Judgement…?" Wheezed the Head Librarian.

"My Judgement is that if she finds herself interested in an unstable life of constant travel, a life with no home, a difficult and occasionally dangerous life, but a free and purposeful one, then she is fit to be my Apprentice, and I would offer her the position should she desire it."

Aeda gasped, reeling backward in surprise. The Head Librarian threw his hands up and grit his teeth. "Gieral, you… why… you… you are the most ridiculous, most troublesome, most irritating, most… Why would you not just say that you planned to make her your Apprentice? Why put us through this ridiculous process at all?"

"She stole from a Historian, therefore a Judgement was mandated. And Historians do not have the power to simply make someone their Apprentice. It is an offer that must be accepted."

"You could have at least told me your intention! Or, better still, told her of your intention! Stick to the rules like a drunk to ale, but in the absence of them, you're as carefree and wild as a babe running naked through a field. Namuor knows why you became a Historian; you should be on a street corner in

Amrodesa telling jokes."

"Do you agree with this Judgement, Head Librarian?" Asked Gieral.

"Well, of course, how silly this has all been. Aedreana, would you want to be a Historian's Apprentice? Keep in mind it will be as *this* Historian's Apprentice; you will deal with this damnable woman for years. Oh, and, erm, no more thieving, of course."

Sleepless nights, angry spirits, brigands, a run in with a loathsome Identifier… Yet I never lacked for food, unlike Braedyn she took notice of my existence, and freedom from the Society. A life of excitement and a life with meaning.

"Yes."

CHAPTER

TWELVE

The Head Librarian chased drops of sweat from his forehead with a tiny pocket square. "How fitting that Gieral takes a Thief for her Apprentice. Or should I say former Thief? Not much chance of going back to the Grey Society now. The last thing for you, Aedreana, is to swear an oath to your mentor, and in turn she will swear her oath to you."

"I'm not sure what to say," Aeda faltered, her head reeling.

"Well, I will make it easy then," calmed the Head Librarian. "Aedreana of Biersport, do you pledge to follow Gieral as your guide and mentor, to learn from her as you embrace the path of a Historian?"

"Yes," Aeda resolutely affirmed.

Gieral smiled. "And I, Historian, Gieral of the Moor, Mark of the White Crane, take Aedreana of Biersport as my Apprentice. I pledge to guide her with dignity, conviction, and integrity as I teach her the ways of the Historians."

Relief washed over Aeda like a cool breeze on a warm summer day. A whirling mirage of emotions overcame her, but before she could form a coherent thought, the Head Librarian grumbled loudly. "Iyra, we know you're there."

Iyra entered gingerly from a shadowed alcove. "Sorry, I didn't think you would hear me."

"You are apologizing for the wrong thing," scolded the Head Librarian. "Judgements are supposed to be private."

"Sorry for…"

"Why even bother apologizing at this point? It has become rather expected and we know you are not truly sorry," mused the Head Librarian. "You may as well be a cat, Iyra, always snooping around, poking your nose in everything. I don't think I should be surprised if you start knocking books and scrolls off shelves. Well, since you're here, why don't you take Miss Aedreana and give her a more formal tour of the library? Go on you two, I have other matters to discuss with Gieral. Oh, Iyra, it would make sense for you to take her to the Quartermaster first, gather her things and then you can show her the rest of the library. Off you are then."

Aeda was in a daze, wanting both to scream with joy and collapse in relief. Iyra gave Aeda time for neither, grabbing her hand. The Librarian beamed as they raced down the halls. "Congratulations! It is so exciting that you are an Apprentice Historian, to Gieral no less. I thought she would never take an Apprentice."

"Why is that?"

"She's such an… independent person. I can't recall ever seeing her arrive or leave with another person. Even though most of the Historians take on Apprentices, and many travel with companions, it didn't seem like her style. What was it like traveling with her?"

"It was interesting, to say the least."

The Librarian carried on excitedly. "You must tell me all about it! Er, please, and if you don't mind?"

Storytelling was far from Aeda's most favored activity, yet Iyra was an enthusiastic listener making the recounting of her travels tolerable, if not enjoyable. Aeda was describing the noisy village of Crost when they arrived at the storehouse. Despite having lived in a city which served as a trade hub, she had never seen such a well-supplied storage. Behind a counter were rows of shelves neatly packed with practical items such as clothes and hatchets and satchels, and also seemingly superfluous toys and musical instruments.

"Quartermaster!" Iyra exclaimed, clapping her hands on the counter.

"Iyra!" came the reply as a book was shut to mimic the sound of the Librarian's thumping hands. A lithe Spriggan marched out from the shelves, her tabard embroidered with a leaf on a barrel. The woman was short, with a sepia complexion, large eyes perched atop high cheekbones, her ears sloping to a short point. Aeda was captivated by the Quartermaster's horns, which were capped with colorful woven ornaments.

The woman leaned on the counter, her voice carrying feigned seriousness. "Have you come to stir up trouble in my little domain? And who have you brought with you, Iyra? Hopefully, she knows better than to associate with a troublemaker like you."

Iyra laughed heartily. "This is Aeda. She used to be a Thief in Biersport, but now she is Apprentice to Gieral. She has had the most wonderful travels! Gieral gave her a cloak and shoes, but she needs practically everything else for an Apprentice."

"How did you know she gave me those things?" Aeda inquired. "I didn't tell you and no one mentioned them during the Judgement."

Iyra's face flushed with horror. "I am terribly sorry… Last night I may have communed with the Runetree after you and Gieral left. I couldn't help myself; I was too curious."

"You will find that Librarians can be quite nosy. We're isolated from the rest of the world and don't have many secrets between us. I'm sure Iyra didn't mean anything by her reading, though as we have learned," the Quartermaster said to the Librarian, "it is usually best to learn personal things from a person directly rather than sneaking around to have a little midnight read. That said, we must properly outfit our friend Gieral's new Apprentice! Follow me and we will gather what you need. No need to thieve or pay, it is all free for Historians."

The Quartermaster opened a hinged section of the counter and invited the girls to join her. She took a floppy canvas sack from a hook on the wall and strode into the rows of shelves.

"Iyra said that Gieral gave you shoes. You seem to have lost them."

"They're dirty. I didn't want to wear them to the Judgement."

"Well, you need shoes, and it won't hurt to have more than one pair. You can wash the others later. In the meantime, put these on." The Quartermaster tossed a pair of boots to Aeda. "If those don't fit, I'll resign from my post."

Aeda slipped into the leather shoes, a perfect fit.

"Which color would you like?" the Quartermaster asked, motioning to shelves lined with earth toned essence pouches with colorful stitching and polished metal buckles.

"I'm not quite sure," replied Aeda, not used to being offered a choice.

"You can think on it. We'll come back."

Continuing down the other aisles, the Quartermaster filled the sack with clothes: a thick fur cloak, a scarf, gloves, and a mottled light orange and red tabard with white embroidery of an open tome over a Runetree. She slowed as they came to an aisle with musical instruments, cards, and other pastime trinkets.

"How did you spend your idle time in Biersport?" inquired the Quartermaster. "Historians occasionally find themselves unoccupied and you will want things to keep yourself entertained. Quiet evenings around campfires or some such. I much prefer my nights in a warm bed with a fire in the hearth, but to each their own."

"I watched ships in the harbor and made these," responded Aeda, raising her arm, seashell bracelets sliding on her wrist.

The Quartermaster deposited a spyglass, a ball of leather cord, a few palm-sized cloth bags filled with glass and metal beads, a small wooden box with a brass key, and a flute in the sack.

"I can't play the flute," Aeda cautioned.

"And? Just because you cannot play now does not mean you cannot learn," retorted the Quartermaster. "You weren't an Apprentice yesterday, and you might not have thought you could ever be one, but today here you are. Yesterday's inability defines neither today's opportunity nor tomorrow's possibility. The flute is a nice instrument and I think you should learn it. It may surprise you how music can open hearts and minds."

"But how will I learn?"

"That will be Gieral's concern. And likely her earache as well.

Now, that should be everything you need for the time being, except for your essence pouches."

The Quartermaster marched back through the stores to a section of essence pouches which seemed to best match the Apprentice's size. Aeda instead halted a few steps away and pulled out a long, dark chocolate brown leather belt with taupe stitching.

"Those are going to fall off you. The belt is far too big," chided the Quartermaster.

"But you did say I could pick one of the color I would like. It might not fit today, but perhaps tomorrow it will be possible for it to fit," Aeda sassed.

Iyra snorted back a giggle as the Quartermaster squinted. "Toss it in, then, and you two can be on your way. If you ever feel you are missing something, come back and see me and we will set you straight. I'm sure we will meet again before you depart, whenever that might be."

They thanked the Quartermaster and set out from the storeroom, Aeda lugging the nearly bursting sack.

"I truly am sorry for digging into your past," apologized Iyra.

"If you already knew, then why did you ask me to tell you about my travels?" Replied Aeda, more surprised that anyone would be interested in her than irritated.

"It is much more interesting to hear stories firsthand! I like hearing what people feel is worth mentioning or what details they leave out. It was rude of me though. Perhaps I can make amends. I could teach you to play the flute?"

Aeda smiled at the prospect as they deposited the trove of new belongings in her quarters. The rest of the day was a whirlwind as Iyra whisked Aeda across the Great Library, chatting away the entire time.

They first went to the Training Room. Rush mats loosely divided the room into practice areas. A countless variety of wooden weapons were organized in racks along the back wall.

"I didn't think Librarians would be fighters," said Aeda.

"We are caretakers of the Runetrees, which means not only managing the recordings but also protecting them from any threat."

"What about the city guards?"

"Their job is to defend the city, but it is our responsibility to safeguard the Runetrees. Being honest, it's not my favorite. I don't think I've ever heard of someone harming a Runetree. Who would even consider it?"

They watched two Librarians spar, one carrying a spear with a blunted tip and the other wielding a limber sword. Aeda's heart rushed at the punctuated cracks of the weapons. A swing of the spear blew back her hair. She thought of Gieral's brusque style, quite different from the fluid Librarians. They leapt and slid, a graceful show of acrobatics intermingled with deadly thrusts and swings.

Strike after strike and parry after parry, the Librarians carried on until they were dripping with sweat. The display enthralled Aeda, though a sideward glance revealed a disinterested Iyra, the young Librarian giving more attention to picking at a loose thread on her tabard than the athletic display. The sparring Librarians closed with a respectful bow, prompting Iyra and Aeda to continue the tour.

They took a side passage to the kitchens, scrumptious smells reaching Aeda long before they arrived. A dozen Librarians were hard at work; they roasted quarters of goat on a spit, broiled sweet jam, kneaded balls of dough, and sliced vegetables by the bucketful.

"Most Librarians spend some time helping in the kitchens, but there are two head chefs. At least one of them is always here, ensuring we all cook to their standard," Iyra noted. Aeda was thankful for everyone involved in the preparations, reminiscing about the prior night's dinner. *I'll be happy to volunteer my time here if I can learn to be half the cook these chefs are.*

She happily filled her belly on a lunch of charred meat and thick slices of hearty black bread leftover from breakfast, accompanied with braised vegetables in a pleasantly tangy sauce. Iyra swiped two fruit tarts as they departed, laughing and tossing one to Aeda.

They pushed open two ochre doors to an extensive study with tidy rows of tall shelves filled with books, scrolls, vials, jars, and plants in clay pots. There were pockets of Librarians sitting at stone tables throughout, some intently reading alone while others chatted zealously in groups. Two white-haired Librarians roamed the sanctum, occasionally chiming in with advice.

"This is the Runewriting Hall," explained Iyra. "As the name suggests, you'll learn to runewrite here."

"Why do Librarians wear so many different tabards?" Aeda asked, noting the two elder Librarians' tabards emblazoned with a pattern of runes forming a tree.

"Our tabards display our standing, and for senior Librarians, their role," responded Iyra. "Our youngest initiates have a single leaf, trainees a branch with leaves, assistants such as myself have a fledgling tree, and finally graduated Librarians have a Runetree. Those with specialized roles receive a unique tabard. The runes forming a tree on those two's tabards to show that they are runewriting mentors."

From the Runewriting Hall, Iyra took an abrupt turn, leading down a stairway carved from the trunk of a single enormous tree. Nearing the end of the steps, Aeda heard clangs of hammers pounding metal. A gust of warm damp air reminded her of summer in Biersport.

They arrived at the Craftworks, a vast space with thick stone columns supporting the high ceiling. It was oddly bright despite a lack of windows, rune-lit sconces lining walls and pillars providing ample light. Huge shelves housed materials from untreated hides to planks of wood to bolts of fine cloth. Aeda spied the source of the heat in one corner, an open forge with bellows so large they took two Librarians to operate. There were vents cut in the walls behind the furnace, though Aeda doubted their effectiveness as a fresh wave of hot air blew from the bellows. Librarians were busy hammering metal, carving wood, and stitching cloth and leather at worktables.

"Most everything you saw in the storehouse came from here," Iyra commented. "You can learn to craft whatever you fancy, from a flute to a satchel."

Looking at the shelves of masterfully crafted goods, Aeda felt shy about her own bracelets. She would have been content to watch the Librarians work for hours, but Iyra delayed only briefly. Down a hall of dark grey brick, they passed by dozens of wooden doors, each leading to a private sanctuary for Librarians and Historians to use when they desired quietude. Iyra pointed to barred metal doors which flanked the end of the hall, each leading to the city through tunnels. Librarians used the underpasses to discreetly bring in supplies without the commotion of going through the front of the Great Library.

At the end of the hall was a tranquil room with a round pool in the center. Aeda marveled at the mosaic of a white tree in a rainbow of colorful tiles which lined the bottom. Dozens of spouts fed the pool, each fashioned to look like a leaf dripping from a spring rain.

"That door over there leads to pumps that take water to the washrooms and the kitchens. Aside from the gardens outside, that's the Great Library," concluded Iyra.

"It's beautiful," said Aeda. "You're lucky to call this place home."

"I suppose it's alright," Iyra said flatly.

"How can you say that? The library is extraordinary. I used to live in a cistern."

"That sounds exciting!" Iyra recoiled on seeing Aeda's furrowed brow. "I mean, I'm not ungrateful; I envy Historians a little is all. Maybe it's good for Librarians and Historians to be a bit jealous of each other. Anyhow, supper will be served soon. We can help prepare!"

Aeda happily followed to the dining hall to assist the bustling Librarians. Over dinner, Iyra asked an endless string of questions about Biersport, life as a Thief, and travels with Gieral. Bellies full, they leisurely returned to the Historian quarters.

"Thank you," Aeda mumbled, shifting awkwardly. *What else should I say? How could such a doomed day turn pleasant?*

Iyra smiled broadly. "It was my pleasure; I hope I haven't

worn out my welcome. As long as you are here, and for as long as you would like, I'll be your guide. I'll see you in the morning to help you get situated with your training. Sleep well!"

Aeda was more worn out than if she had spent the whole day traveling, but her heart felt lifted above the highest trees in Amrodesa. Gieral sat at one of the small tables reading a scroll. Aeda gave an unsure bow, then rolled onto her own bed, releasing a contented sigh.

"You don't have to be formal with me," said Gieral, unmoved from her scroll. "We are partners now. You should, however, continue bowing to Librarians and other Historians. It is the polite thing to do. Look by your bed there, on the ledge."

She certainly is the strangest woman. In a square cubbyhole in the wall sat a grey scabbard, its hardened leather enrobed in delicate, intertwined steel ribbons. At the mouth rested a thin crossguard framing a handle of braided black strips of leather. The pommel was an orb of steel carved with a ring of thorned vines and flowers. Aeda grasped the handle and drew the dagger. A ridge ran from the crossguard to the tip, dividing the blade into a matte half with fine stippling in the metal, and a polished half bearing an indented black stem and flower.

"A dagger is a useful tool, and as you have seen, the road can be somewhat dangerous," Gieral said. "Now that you're an Apprentice Historian, it is fitting for you to carry something a touch dignified."

"Thank you," Aeda replied as she admired the blade, slowly turning it in the candlelight. She felt her mentor was belittling the quality of the gift. She had once stolen a dagger crusted in gems, but it seemed a gaudy bauble compared to the blade she now held. "Why were you in Biersport?"

"The more we travel, the more you will understand what drives Historians to their destinations. As for why I was traveling to Biersport in particular… well, seeing as you are my Apprentice, I shouldn't keep secrets. I will be forward with you. I have a suspicion that Historians are disappearing. Not hearing from a Historian for a long time is common, and an older Historian retiring to their homeland or occasionally meeting an untimely end on the road isn't unheard of, but I believe these disappearances to be different. I was hoping to meet with the Council of the Grey Society in case they might know something. Sending Thieves to steal from me was a rather clear message that they did not want to chat."

"What do you mean, disappearing Historians? And you know the Council? I thought no one except the Attendants had ever met them."

"Disappearing might be an overly strong statement. If it was one or two Historians with an extended absence, it would not be cause for alarm, but there is an uncomfortable trend of silence. Simply, too many have not been seen for too long. As for the Council, to say I know them would be a stretch. As you are aware, they are quite secretive. Let's call it a passing familiarity. But you need not worry about my suspicions. You will find them quite unpopular with Librarians and Historians alike. Your focus should be expressly on your training."

Not wanting to irritate her new mentor, Aeda pivoted her questioning. "Ferin said you removed the Grey Society's binding. Why did you say that you were binding me to you?"

"Every Thief, no matter their age, is rune-bound to the will of the Grey Society. Did you ever wonder why, despite your unhappiness, you never seriously considered leaving Biersport, perhaps even fearing the idea? The Society does not like its servants having the option to stray. My deception was in part a test for you and also a convenience for me. I was curious to see how you would react, and toting you bound in chains was completely impractical."

She removed my binding and set me free from the Grey Society; what then drove me to return? The spirit wasn't summoned by Gieral, but something compelled me to return...

"Now, that is enough questions for tonight. Rest. The next few weeks will be quite busy with your training, tomorrow no exception."

Gieral's last few words fell on deaf ears as Aeda had already drifted to sleep.

CHAPTER

THIRTEEN

Aeda woke to see Gieral sitting at her table, reading as if she had not moved since the prior night. "Good morning. I believe Iyra is already waiting for you in the dining hall. You should get to it; you have a full day ahead."

Aeda splashed her face with water and ran out of the room. Speeding through the halls, she cut around corners, kicking off the walls, startling more than one Librarian as she darted through passageways. Spilling into the dining hall, Aeda came to an abrupt stop in a seat across from Iyra.

"Am I late?" Aeda wheezed.

"No, not at all. I am glad to see you!" Iyra cheerily greeted.

"Oh, I thought I was late. Are there others joining us too?"

"Just you and me. Most of the Historians' training takes place as they travel with their mentor. It is unusual to have more than one or two Apprentice Historians at a time learning in the Great Library."

After a meal of herbaceous rice porridge, split top oat bread and fruit, the two proceeded to Namuor's chamber. Sensing her counterpart's apprehension, Iyra grabbed Aeda's hand and skipped the rest of the way, laughing while Aeda hesitantly trotted alongside her.

Aeda froze upon seeing the inexplicably marvelous Namuor again. Before, runes seemed to surround the Runetree, yet now it was clear they were as much a part of the Runetree as its leaves and roots, flowing in and out of seams in the trunk like a breeze through a lace curtain.

While she admired the ivory runes, an older man sporting a trim silver beard approached. Wrinkled and weathered skin framed his eyes, which brimmed with content.

"Welcome, Iyra, and Aeda I presume?" He invited, his voice rich like toffee dipped in warm chocolate. "I am Roswalt, and it would seem I have been tasked with telling you about Runetrees and what it means to be a Historian."

Iyra bowed, though Aeda forewent the gesture and spoke directly. "Are you a Librarian or a Historian? Your tabard isn't blue or red."

"Astute," replied Roswalt, patting his green tabard with an intricate tome stitched in the center. "I am a retired Historian, too old to travel but young enough to spend my days fussing around, bothering Librarians. Once in a while, I put myself to use and help train Apprentice Historians and the occasional wayward Librarian. Come, let us sit and we will discover what I can still remember. Iyra, you are welcome to join us. You know much of what we will discuss, but a reminder would not hurt."

"Why not commune directly with Runetrees?" Aeda asked.

"You will not be rid of me so easily," laughed Roswalt. "There are a few reasons. The most important being that it takes a good deal of practice before you will be capable enough to effectively commune on your own. Even then, you would lack direction on where to start and which events are of interest. It helps to know what you are looking for when communing and Runetrees are not the type to answer questions, which I am happy to do."

They followed Roswalt up a spiraling set of white stone stairs. Aeda had not realized there was a proper second floor, complete with oval seating nooks overlooking Namuor. Sliding onto a bench, Roswalt began the lesson.

"I think first we should talk about the prevalence of Runetrees. I'm sure Gieral already gave you some introduction as to their purpose. Now, you must understand that Runetrees are not regular trees bound in runes. They are a living, breathing record of history. Did Gieral tell you about how the Runetrees were spread across the Known Lands?"

"Yes, cuttings from Namuor were carried to found the first cities."

"A fair foundation. Did she talk about why the Runetrees look the way they do? No? A good place to start, then. The first cuttings of Namuor were little more than twigs when first planted, all identical in appearance. Over time, as years went by, they changed, and continue to change, every day. By change, I mean not only in the history recorded within, but also in their physical form. Not a single Runetree in all the Known Lands looks at all like this magnificent specimen. The same is true for smaller Runetrees. They might bear some resemblance to the Runetree from which they were cut, but I assure you when they were first planted, they looked identical to their parent tree for many, many years."

Though the lesson was informative and Roswalt a riveting

speaker, Aeda was unused to sitting idly. Her legs bounced, fingers fidgeting as she scanned the white stone pillars. Braedyn had always been brief in his talks, telling her the least amount necessary in the shortest time possible before going off on his own way. Even in quiet moments, she watched ships in the harbor or people in the markets and would roam as she pleased. This seat was foreign and restrictive, and it was as if the walls were squeezing in like a collapsing cage which…

"Aeda?"

The absent-minded Apprentice murmured an embarrassed apology.

"No need to be sorry," replied Roswalt, rising with a knowing smile. "You are going to be a Historian, not a statue. No need to count sitting around and listening to lectures to be among your strengths. Come, you can listen as we walk. I know Iyra is not one to enjoy sitting for long periods of time, either. Oh, and this should help."

He fished from a pocket a small metal sphere with three intersecting rings evenly spaced around its circumference, dividing the ball into eight equal wedges. He showed how the gears spun around the sphere, the wedges shifting and blending in colorful shades. "This will keep your hands occupied. If you're able to achieve one color across all the sections, the puzzle ball will open, and you will find a little prize inside."

For the better part of the morning, Iyra and Aeda roamed the library with Roswalt. She thought the puzzle orb might distract her, but found that occupied hands aided her focus. Roswalt spoke further about the variations of Runetrees, such as the one in Biersport. Its windswept appearance was a result not of years exposed to the wind and salt air, instead, it was from the weathering of the city itself. He shared how many small villages had their own Runetree, cuttings taken by Librarians on request. In some cases, individuals might even request a branch to plant by their home, providing a personal view of the passage of time.

"I think I have bored you enough for today," said Roswalt, having led the girls halfway around the library and back again. "You have other instructors to see."

"Not a bore at all!" chimed Iyra.

"Thank you," responded Aeda, tucking the puzzle orb into a pocket.

"We'll see if you still thank me after lessons in a week's time," he chuckled in departure.

"Where to next?" Asked Aeda.

"I think it's time to get your essence pouches."

Aeda took the lead, suppressing her desire to run through the halls. In the Historian chambers, she threw the essence pouches around her waist and cinched the belt down. It fell askew, slipping low when she took a step towards the door. Cursing the Quartermaster for being right, Aeda slung the belt over her shoulder and strode to the Runewriting Hall.

As Aeda and Iyra entered, a Librarian approached; finely sewn runes in the shape of a sapling emblazoned her tabard. Narrow wrinkles creased in the corners of the Librarian's eyes as she brushed a lock of salted-and-peppered auburn hair aside. "Aeda, it's my pleasure to meet you. My name is Delia. I'll be teaching you the fundamentals of runewriting. Iyra, you're quite familiar with these lessons. Perhaps you can come back when it is time for lunch."

"Of course," Iyra said with a bow.

The Librarian guided Aeda to a bulky stone table flanked by high-backed wooden chairs. Five cylindrical glass jars sat in a row, each as large as a pumpkin and topped with a cork. Sparkling, undulating rune essence filled each. Motioning Aeda to a seat beside her, Delia slid over the jar filled with a light silver-grey essence. The glass scraped on the coarse table, and a horrible shriek echoed through the hall. Aeda's hands snapped over her ears, though the Librarian seemed unaffected and grinned blankly.

"It would be a lie to say these are high-quality essences, but they are absolutely perfect for training. And trust me on the quality, I made these," said Delia, eyes darting between the jars and the Apprentice. "Do you know how essences are made?"

"No," came Aeda's hushed reply. The pulsing fluid drew her back to the fateful day in Biersport, spent staring at Gieral's life essences.

"A quick background and then we'll get to practice. Rune essences are not harvested from some fantastical source, rather, they are a mixture of reagents and fragments of a person's soul. I suppose the first part of what I said was not exactly true as pieces of our souls are fantastic and extraordinary, but the reagents are not *necessarily* exciting. Well, sometimes reagents can be harvested from a fantastical source, but not always.

"Anyway, we will get into more about the reagents and soul fragments in the coming days. Suffice it to say, the process of crafting rune essence can be quite tiring and requires a great deal of personal investment, given you are carving off bits of your soul. Now the potency of rune essence depends on the quality of reagents, but also on the skill of the person crafting the essence. Some skilled essence crafters have become quite wealthy for their abilities, while reagent hunters have found fortune gathering rare and powerful reagents. Riches aside—and don't be thinking about riches as Librarians and Historians alike aren't in it for wealth—there are six types of essences, each with a range of possible reagents used to create them."

"If there are six types, then why are there only five jars on the table?" Aeda asked.

"I'll describe the six and then it should be quite clear why we only have five." Prying off the cork lid from the stormy grey essences, Delia pointed the tip of her stylus over the jar, circling gently above. The pulsing essences stiffened, swirling rhythmically and trailing the stylus. The Librarian reached for Aeda's waist where the essence pouches should be. Delia's eyes bounced from Aeda's shoulder to her waist and back. The Librarian shrugged and flipped open one of Aeda's essence pouches and pointed into it with her stylus, a thin stream of the essence filling it like honey in a pot.

"The first type of essence is the easiest to create, air essence." Delia's gaze flitted about the room as she spoke. "The reagent is one of the more interesting, as you can create air essence anywhere. Well, almost anywhere, I suppose you couldn't make air essences underwater. Not the prime place to be making essences in any case. *Ahem*, the air around a crafter will dictate the nature of the essence. Thundering storms on mountain peaks create the perfect environment for the most potent of air essences, while the stagnant, ancient air of caves, deep underground, result in the most pure essence. Air runes can manipulate the world in the same way you might imagine a strong, focused wind could. You can create a breeze or move an object from one place to another with these runes."

Once the pouch was full, Delia flicked her stylus over the jar and the essences returned to an oozing flow. The Librarian repeated the transfer process with a jar of emerald-green essences. "Second are earth essences, crafted with organic matter. Leaves, soil, rocks, and many other materials serve as reagents for earth essence. The reagents change the nature of the essence like herbs changing the flavor of a dish."

"Could you use part of a Runetree to create earth essences?" Aeda asked.

"Can you? Yes. Should you? No. Will you? Absolutely not on my watch. Grinding a piece of a Runetree to powder and using the dust results in exceptionally potent essence, but for the respect of history, the importance of Runetrees, and the instability of the result, even the most reckless of essence crafters deem it unwise. Earth runes are some of the most widely used. With the right earth runeword, a gardener can increase a plant's yield tenfold." The Librarian sealed the jar, transitioning to a blue jar.

"Third are water essences, the name an obvious indicator of the source. These have the unique distinction of being used to transfer recordings from tomes to Runetrees. Watering the greenery, if you will. You will find using pure spring water from high on a mountain will result in much better essences than pulling water from a latrine. Before you ask, yes, some mischievous young Librarians thought it would be humorous to try. Trust me, the essence did not function well, and the smell lingered for days."

"Is there a difference between water from, say, the ocean or a river?"

"An excellent question. There are subtle effects. The function of essence depends not only on the skill of the person crafting; their background also matters. You might find salt water a more natural reagent to work with given you lived in Biersport, but there is no way to know until you try. These have two common uses. First is for healing, which in times of peace is a lesser appreciated but still a valuable capability. Second is to supplement any situation water might be involved, such as watering fields in a drought. They are my favorite, so you will start with these today.

"Fourth are flame essences, or fire essences. They are one and the same, typically created with ashes or hot coals. Though challenging, it is possible to create flame essences from a burning fire. You will have a much better product if you find charred remains from a wyrm fire or some other interesting event as opposed to ash from a hearth in some backwater inn. There is a caveat to that. If someone crafts essences using ashes from a place that has great meaning for them or right after some notable event, the results can still be quite potent. I would be quite surprised if you have not yet seen Gieral start a fire with a flame rune."

"Yes, more than once."

"She had better not be showing off. Essences are expensive, and she is capable of making a fire with her hands too. Well then, fifth, and final of the acceptable essences, are life essences, which I understand you have some fleeting familiarity with." Delia was oblivious as Aeda groaned at the slight. "These are unique in that the reagent is also soul fragments, meaning it takes two people to create life essences. Based on the relationship of the source, whether dear friends, lovers, business partners, competitors, or foes, the nature of the essence may change drastically. Master essence crafters charge handsomely to create life essences with buyers, whereas Historians and Librarians create them together. Life runes can be tricky to use properly as they usually have some personal or emotional effect, like bindings. Though most would hardly consider bindings a proper use of runes."

"And what is the sixth?" Aeda inquired, the last of her essence pouches full.

"Sixth are death essences." Delia paused after shutting the purple jar. "Have you experienced death before? Excuse me, the question should be, have you been around death before? If you had experienced death, we would not likely be chatting now."

"Yes, once," replied Aeda.

"So, you have some familiarity with the unfortunate and unpleasant nature of death. Good. That's not good. I mean, it is good for our discussion, but not good as in… what I mean is, you understand. It might not be evident from your experience but when a person or creature dies, there are fleeting moments at their end, when the mind and body have resigned themselves to fate, where the last vestiges of life, bits of their soul, cling to the corpse and linger.

"Death essences are crafted by extracting the remaining fragments of a nearly dead being's soul, sealing their fate. The whole bit about finalizing the end of a life, sealing the deal, making something *absolutely* dead, has led to their rarity. Not only is the collection a nasty process, death runes are only used to inflict harm. Sure, you can hurl a ball of fire at someone or fill their lungs with water or slash them with a blade of air or crush them in constricting vines, but at least the other essences are generally used for pleasant purposes.

"Anyhow! Let us move on to the lesson at hand. Your essence pouches are full, next is your stylus. You can use most any object in a pinch, from a twig to a skinny piece of stone, though what you use for a stylus may affect your runes. I once used a chicken bone to light a fire. The flames gave off such a delectable aroma. You're welcome to pick whatever you want; a stylus is a personal instrument. The more you use it, the more it will grow with you and etchings will appear based on how you use it. I have brought a stylus for you to use until you find whatever you deem to suit you best. If it happens to work for you, that's fine too. Some Librarians continue to use the first stylus they received."

Aeda took the rowan stylus and traced a finger across its finely polished surface. Meanwhile, Delia procured a thick, tattered book and a grey cloak.

"I'm of the belief it's important to learn by doing. You'll start by imbuing this cloak to reflect water. Simple but useful, especially for Historians who are often on the road, no roof overhead, exposed to the battering winds and rain and hail, the tempests that soak and chill and steal away all sense of joy and hope. Who knows when such a storm might roll in? Read this."

Flipping open the cover, Delia turned to an early page. On the left was a block of text and a diagram of a runeword with instructions for each arc and line, while the right depicted a man wearing a cloak with comically large water droplets bouncing off. Aeda skimmed over the text and raised her stylus, eager to try the runeword.

"Ready then? Open your water essence pouch. Gently lower the tip of your stylus until it barely touches the surface of the essences; you don't want to dunk the end in, or your runeword will be clumsy. The writing sets the stage for the result. Runewriting is all about grace. A soft touch means a strong rune, so they say. Or at least so I say. Go ahead, write the runeword, in the air between you and the cloak."

Nodding, Aeda mindfully traced the runes to match the example presented in the book. "Next?" She inquired; her hand frozen at the end of the runeword.

"Next, you strike the runeword. Bring your arm across your chest until the back end of the stylus hangs by your left shoulder. Good. Now, carefully, bring the tip of the stylus through the heart of the runes as you swing your hand to the right."

Aeda slowly brought her arm up to the described position, focusing on the runeword in front of her. In a flash, she flung her stylus through the runes. The essence blasted forth with a crack and the cloak shot over shelves and across the room as if flung by an Ogre.

"I'm so sorry!" Aeda exclaimed with a grimace. To her relief, the Librarians were too occupied with their own studies to notice.

"Not a trouble. Wait here," Delia chortled as she rose in pursuit. She returned carrying the cloak and an ewer of water. Aeda surveyed the cloak as Delia set it on the table, hoping to see some change, but the garment was as mundane as before. Delia coyly smiled. "Let's see the result of your first, and most energetic, runeword."

Lifting the ewer dramatically above the cloak, Delia tilted the vessel, releasing a thin stream of water. Expecting a splash, Aeda recoiled and covered her face with her hand. Peering between her disappointingly dry fingers, her face drooped. Delia snickered and emptied the entire contents of the vessel into the cloak.

"What happened? Why did it fail?" Aeda scowled, hardly believing what she saw.

"To be fair, your runeword not only failed, it completely reversed. You imbued the cloak to absorb an enormous amount of water instead of repelling it," replied Delia. The Librarian lifted the cloak and gave it a solid shake, not a single drop falling away. "You certainly wrote a potent runeword. Do you understand why it didn't have the intended effect?"

"No, I think I wrote the runes properly, I obviously didn't have issues with striking it, I did what the book said," Aeda fumed.

"I should have explained better. Runewriting is not a skill of dexterity. Your writing is quite nice though, more than sufficient. You should see the Head Librarian's handwriting. It's atrocious. Runewriting has to come from the heart and the mind, and the thoughts you carry are even more important than the motion of your hands. When you cast a rune to imbue a cloak to repel water, you shouldn't be thinking about how a cloak would otherwise absorb water, which is what I'm guessing was running through your mind. You need to feel the water bouncing off, fleeing the surface, scrambling to stay away from the cloth. When you master what goes on in your head, your runes will gain much greater potency."

"It's much different than I thought it would be," Aeda moped.

"All you need is practice. Your runeword was powerful, and in achieving the opposite of the intended effect, you can only get better. I have plenty more cloaks for you to work with. Or maybe we should try with a towel next time… Just as well, there's more than one shop which might consider this a nice curiosity to add to their stock. Don't fret, we have plenty of time to turn you into a capable runewriter. I see Iyra is here anyhow. No one can learn properly on an empty stomach. Off you go. Eat!"

CHAPTER

FOURTEEN

Iyra sat across from Aeda, momentarily content with being quiet in the warm afternoon. A hefty platter with thinly sliced golden wheat bread, rich red berry jam, strips of grilled squash, and beets drizzled with sweet honey adorned the board. Aeda woke from her daze and tucked in with an unrealized hunger.

"How was runewriting?" Iyra tepidly ventured.

Halfway through a bite, Aeda coughed. "Disappointing. I tried to make a cloak repel water, except instead of repelling water, it absorbed it. Delia emptied an entire jug into the cloak and not a drop touched the ground."

"The first time I tried runewriting, absolutely nothing happened. I felt awful, it was a complete failure! I still struggle with runewriting."

"I thought all Librarians and Historians must be masters of it," said Aeda. "It seems effortless for Gieral."

"I have to practice constantly, and I'm sure Gieral uses runes all the time. A little secret, Librarians don't have to write runes except for when we record to Runetrees. Not everyone

✦ 126 ✦

is as practiced as you might think. Did you decide on what to use for a stylus?"

"Delia gave me this," Aeda said, showing Iyra the stylus. "It's beautiful. I should use it."

"I'm sure you have something more interesting and exciting," encouraged Iyra, sensing hesitancy. "When I began runewriting, I knew I would ultimately use something different. I was told that if I wanted something else, it would be best to use something that had meaning for me. I use a tuning peg from a lute since I love music."

"I wish it was simpler." Aeda stewed in frustration. *At least thieving had come naturally to me.*

"This is your first day! I'm sure you'll be a master in no time."

They went to the Craftworks after lunch, where a stout Librarian with a smudge on her cheek and frizzy, unkempt black hair was waiting at a sturdy table surrounded by stools. A tree bordered by a multitude of small symbols adorned her tabard, among them a fire and a hatchet.

"I'm Bula. I teach Apprentice Historians the basics of surviving in the wild." The Librarian's voice was thick, dry, and uneven, like a hunk of stale bread crumbling when squeezed. "While Librarians hide away in the nicest parts of cities, Historians have the pleasure of spending a considerable amount of time in the less hospitable areas between those nice places. Since I know you will ask why a Librarian would teach Historians, I spent years adventuring before becoming a Librarian. You will get plenty more from Gieral on the road, but I am here to get you started. Some Historians travel with companions or in groups, which quells some of the risk, but

Gieral is a regular soloist so this will all be relevant."

Bula grumbled at the sight of Aeda's bare feet. "Did the Quartermaster forget to give you shoes?"

"Sorry, I was in a hurry this morning. I thought I was late."

"Well, hurry your feet into shoes next time. You don't want to lose a toe down here. While we are on the topic of housekeeping. I don't like questions, but if you have them, ask anyway. I'm guessing you are joining, Iyra, since you haven't learned any of this. You are, of course, welcome to stay. I will ask that you let the Apprentice ask the questions; if I let you do the asking, we'll be here to the end of time. Now that I've said that, you will probably ask your own questions, anyway. I will be teaching and you will practice your crafting at this table." Bula made a sweeping motion over the empty surface. "Hmph, we may as well gather everything you'll need; it'll save time in the coming days. Follow me!"

They spent the next several hours going back and forth; the Librarian pointed out all manner of goods for the girls to gather. By the end, rope, twine, animal hides, needles, thread, cords of wood, knives, tools of all kinds, bolts of cloth, herbs, seeds, vials, and more covered the table. Aeda and Iyra perched on stools, awaiting instruction. Hand latched to her chin, the Librarian glanced back and forth between the two pupils and the assortment on the table. "You took long enough. We'll start with the actual lessons tomorrow. Whenever you feel up for learning about keeping your hide intact, come down and I'll likely be here. Goodbye."

With that, Bula shuffled away. Iyra rose with a snicker and a shrug. "I suppose we can go to combat training now."

A few Librarians occupied their afternoon sparring in the training rooms. Iyra waved over a behemoth of a man, his broad face sporting a trim, curly tan beard. His graceful movements surprised Aeda, as he glided past with a wide smile. He had rolled up the sleeves of his simple shirt and trousers. "Iyra, it's a rare pleasure to see you here. Are you planning to send me to the infirmary again?"

The sight of Iyra at a loss for words amused Aeda, yet it befuddled her that someone of Iyra's stature could possibly harm the man in front of them.

"Hello, Cordis, this is Aeda. She's the one here to train."

"You should train more often yourself, Iyra. It is a duty of every Librarian," he replied. "And welcome, Aeda."

"How did Iyra best you?" Aeda blurted out.

Cordis chuckled. "I assure you it is true. Best me, she did! In truth, it was a rather embarrassing affair I would rather not revisit. Now to the matter at hand. It's helpful for me to know if you have any experience in combat."

"She took down a runewriter with nothing more than a hatchet!" Iyra enthusiastically interjected.

"They were preoccupied, and I hardly did anything. I just threw my hatchet," Aeda stumbled.

"You addressed a serious threat effectively. A better start than most," reassured Cordis. "Fighting aside, I understand you are quick on your feet and with your hands, which will be useful here. We will not be following some procedural steps of structured and organized training, instead we'll start by sparring and see where best to go from there. Set your things aside and we can begin."

It seems the whole of the Great Library knows I used to be a Thief, Aeda murmured as she stowed her essence pouches in a cubby.

Cordis motioned for her to take her pick from the racks of wooden training weapons. Aeda paced back and forth, studying the dents, cracks, and mars. Weapons of every kind were available, from the simplest of clubs to intricate halberds.

"I don't know where to start."

"You'll eventually try everything. Why not start simple and grab that shortsword? I'll be back in a moment with your sparring partner," said Cordis.

Aeda lifted out a wooden sword, the leather grip large for her hand, but not uncomfortable. She ran her hand along the carved blade, the edges worn smooth and dull. In Cordis's absence, Aeda paced back and forth, wondering who she might spar with. He returned with a red sash tied around his waist.

"What do you think?" He asked, his voice prideful as he picked his own wooden sword.

"It… I guess the color is nice?"

"Oh, that's the best you have to say," he chuckled. "Eventually, I'll teach you techniques to face the beasts and monsters you might find on the road, but let's start with the basics of facing another person, and today, that person is me. Now, for your first lesson, I simply want you to get used to avoiding and striking, balancing the two actions at once. You have three objectives. First, to stay in the marked area for as long as you can; second, strike this cloth as often as you can; while third, be struck as few times as you can. Don't worry about your form for now. Just try to connect that sword with this cloth."

Cordis marked off a circle in the center of the room with a piece of white chalk. Aeda pursed her lips, realizing the Librarian could likely reach the entire circle with his sword if he stood in the middle. Cordis grinned as Aeda stepped into the ring.

"Are you ready?"

"Ye-"

Cordis leapt into motion, catching Aeda's shoulder with the pommel of his sword, knocking her onto her rear and out of the circle. Aeda glared at Cordis as he and Iyra snorted and laughed. Rubbing her arm, she marched back to the ring, determined to best the haughty Librarian. Readied for the assault, she stepped inside.

Cordis sprang forward. With speed exceeding Gieral's, he swung back and forth, swiping and stabbing at Aeda. The frenzied attacks were relentless, sending her rolling, sliding, ducking, spinning, leaping back and forth to avoid the blows. In the incessant flurry, Aeda studied the motions of the Librarian, learning his reach and which strike might come next. Finding a rhythm, she turned her focus to the cloth.

As Cordis brought his sword crashing down to Aeda's left, she lightly stepped right. His foot brushed past her hair as she rolled forward to avoid a kick. Aeda lunged left to avoid a jab from the sword. Cordis reset his stance, poised to strike a retreating prey, but Aeda sprang to the side, kicking off a pillar and nimbly skirting the sword.

Hand outstretched, she yanked the red cloth free of Cordis' waist. Kicking off his shin, she spun backwards. Aeda slid out of the ring and landed deftly in a kneel, hoisting the red cloth in the air. Cordis and Iyra clapped, Aeda beaming.

Cordis smugly placed his hand on Aeda's shoulder. "Iyra was right! You are quite skilled. Though I must say, despite your impressive show, you failed."

Aeda scowled at the thought of having failed for a second time that day. "How so?" She challenged.

Cordis pointed to her sword on the ground. "That is your weapon there. And with it, you struck the cloth precisely zero times."

"But…"

"No need to justify or defend yourself. You did well. My job would be far easier if every Librarian shared your fervor. I am simply reminding you that beyond the walls of the library, you must be mindful of the task at hand. You wouldn't take off your boots and toss them aside while traveling. In the same way, consider your weapon an extension of your body. You never know when a conflict might arise in the wild." Cordis paused for her to consider his words. "I think that is a fine lesson to close the day. I'll see you tomorrow."

Aeda bowed and thanked Cordis.

"How did you learn to move like that?" asked Iyra.

"Stealing and running away," Aeda said. "If you were slow or clumsy, guards would catch you and lock you away in prison. The Society would eventually get us out, but it was far from pleasant rotting there in the meantime. Speaking of unpleasant, how did you manage to send Cordis to the infirmary?"

"I'm not sure how much I should say," said Iyra coolly. "I've never been quick or strong, and combat training is the worst for me. Cordis knew this, and he offered to spend some time exploring other ways of making myself useful. We tried some new techniques, and it turned out to be… well, he ended up in the infirmary. I was told not to mention or attempt those methods again."

Realizing the finality of the statement, Aeda abandoned her curiosity.

The day had passed by in a blink and fatigue washed over Aeda. Inside the chambers, Gieral greeted them from behind a weathered and crinkly scroll. Aeda wondered if her mentor had moved at all, her apparent obsession with relaxing and reading a stark contrast to her pace on the road.

"You two seem to have had a busy day. It is still a short while until supper. Do you have it in you to try one more thing?" asked Gieral.

"I think it might depend on what that thing is," replied Aeda, thinking fondly of the upcoming meal.

"I thought you might try communing."

"Of course!" exclaimed Aeda, standing straight.

Gieral led to a chamber with a smooth barked slate Runetree surrounded with jade runes. The hues entranced Aeda, reminding her of saltwater trapped in tidal pools lit by the moons. Iyra sat on a bench while Gieral and Aeda kneeled beneath the lavender leaves of the Runetree.

"Communing with a Runetree can seem deceptively simple. Making the connection is easy. Controlling the journey through time; that is the challenging part. To begin, I want you to focus on a single event recorded within this Runetree. Do not let your mind stray from that event. Focus on it with every ounce of concentration you have."

"What should I be thinking of?"

"It is easiest to review events you experienced yourself. I want you to find the docks in Biersport the night we met. Think of every detail you can recall, from the feeling of the pier beneath your feet to the sound of the wind to the light of the moons. All you need to do to begin is bring your stylus to the center of your chest and point to the Runetree. This will open the connection between your soul and the Runetree. And remember, do not stop focusing on that night on the docks. Do not let yourself be distracted by the other events you might see."

Aeda admired the fluctuating runes as she took in a deep breath of air. Exhaling, she gripped her stylus, touched it gently to her chest, then directed the instrument to the Runetree. Her eyes snapped shut, and the world dissolved like honey in hot tea, her senses swarmed by an olive-green cloud stirring in her mind. Bright runes appeared to flow through space and time, shapes streaming by and shifting into blurred noises, emotions, and colorful flashes of light.

She thought of the docks, the cloak hanging over Gieral's face, ripples in the ocean, the cool breeze on her cheek. Try as she might to focus, bursting lights distracted her senses, and the memory faded as if a fog blew over the docks. Faster and faster Aeda was propelled through the mist, memories of Biersport blasting by, leaving broken traces of thoughts and emotions she could not process. Countless sounds harmonized into a synchronized drone which pounded in Aeda's ears and colors mixed into an ever brightening white, so bright and loud she could no longer comprehend the meaning of color or sound or touch.

The intensity grew and grew beyond the most intensely

imaginable brilliance, as if she was flying into the sun. When it became so powerful she thought she might burst, Aeda wrenched her eyes open. She saw the Runetree in front of her for a scant moment before collapsing.

CHAPTER

FIFTEEN

Aeda blinked sluggishly, the Runetree replaced by the rafters of the Historian chambers.

"Ah, finally awake," came Gieral's voice. "How are you feeling?"

"Are you alright?" Iyra rushed over.

"I'm fine," Aeda yawned. "Though a little hungry."

"Always food," mused Gieral. "Unfortunately, you missed dinner. Do not fret. Iyra was kind enough to make you something."

"Thank you," said Aeda, eagerly accepting a bowl filled with sliced vegetables, herbs, and thin strips of meat rolled into the shapes of flowers. The broth was still warm, giving off a comforting aroma.

"It was no trouble," said Iyra. "However, it is late. I'll see you in the morning."

Gieral pulled a chair closer as Aeda dove into the flavorful soup. "You are fortunate to have Iyra as a friend. It is not always easy for Historians to find reliable companions."

Aeda gulped and wiped a drop of soup from her chin.

"What happened? Everything went white. It was as if all these memories that weren't mine mixed together and I couldn't make sense of anything."

"That was my mistake, and I must apologize for it. As tired as you were, it was too difficult to focus. When you commune with a Runetree, you are accessing a vault of history, far more history than the sum of all memories in our own minds. Tapping into such an immense recording can overwhelm one's ability to comprehend what they are seeing, leaving them lost among the memories. We will try again in a day or two when you have rested, and I am sure you will have much better results."

"Is it dangerous to lose control?"

"Not particularly. You have experienced the worst that can happen: you faint. Although you are breaking off tiny fragments of your soul as a conduit to communicate with the Runetree."

"I'll recover those fragments, right?"

Gieral grinned at the worry on Aeda's face. "Your soul is the heart of your entire existence. Until you die, your soul will have no trouble healing right back up. All that happens is you feel a bit worn and hungry. Now, finish up, there is something I would like to do before we sleep, and I promise this will be far less taxing."

Aeda followed Gieral to a room with a portly obsidian black Runetree. Deep purple runes covered its bark and circular indigo leaves tipped its branches, each with a cerulean spine that spiraled beyond the tip. The Historian lay under the boughs, streaks of moonlight peeking through the leaves. Aeda plopped, soft tangles of lichens unfurling in a comfortable nest.

"Did Roswalt tell you the story of creation? Or did he jump

in and start talking about how things are today?" Gieral asked.

"He started where you left off. We talked about the way Runetrees look depending on where they are."

"I should have suspected; he's more than once gone round a hill and come stumbling back over the top. Well, now is as good of a time as any. The story of creation begins long ago, before the existence of the Known Lands. In ages past, great beings filled the sky, gods who roamed the endless space above, their existence not bound by rules. Despite this freedom, many were insidious and greedy for power. At first there were minor altercations, but the infighting grew into an outright war which threatened all existence. A few of the gods banded together, determined to stop the conflict. They devised a way to bind their kind and bring an end to their evils."

"How did they capture the rebels?"

"The group seeking peace brought all the gods together under the pretense of selecting an ultimate leader, the god of all gods. In vanity, every single god came, and they sprang the trap. The unified group easily overcame their divided peers, enrobing each of them in an enchanted cloak to bind them into stars and moons. The remaining gods agreed to bind themselves as well, fearful they might one day fall astray. Our sun was one of the unifiers; the world we live on holds the spirit of his wife. The moons in the night sky were their four children. Though the star and his wife were kind, their children were some of the worst instigators in the conflict.

"Because of her good nature and kind spirit, our world became a source of life. Meanwhile, the four jealous children, cold and bitter in the sky, created nothing but evils born of their malcontent, which they sent forth to corrupt their own mother. In response, our star sent the seed of the first Runetree so that we never forget our origins, and that we might turn from the temptations of power. Now Historians and Librarians carry on that purpose, recording and sharing history, that we might learn from those who came before."

"Why did you decide to make me your Apprentice?" Aeda asked.

"After the story of the origin of our world, about inexplicably powerful beings in the sky, you ask why I offered you a place as my Apprentice," Gieral said with feigned incredulity. "If I am truthful, when I first realized you were a Thief in the Grey Society, I had absolutely no intention to make you my Apprentice. I simply acted on the opportunity to remove you from their grasp. It is not a Historian's place to meddle in local affairs, yet I was drawn to you. Perhaps I was motivated in part by my indignation that the Society would dare send their Thieves to steal from a Historian."

"That seems entirely personal."

"Yes, but there was also the formality of the Judgement, which was very much required. Then, quite unexpectedly, our travels opened my eyes to the idea of offering you a place as my Apprentice."

"Aren't you interested in experiencing the places you visit?"

"I do not mean to say we cannot enjoy our travels, but Historians are observers. From Roswalt's lessons in the coming weeks, you will learn that Historians are not compelled to make a momentary difference. Our purpose is a higher one, chronicling history. It would be far too easy for us to abuse our position and the status it affords. We must hold ourselves accountable to our task. History is for us to record, not to create."

"But aren't Historians taking part in history by existing? Why not do more?"

"Yes, but in the context of our ordained role. In being a Historian, wherever you go, you are doing something of note by fulfilling this mandate. You will also come to find that being a Historian affords you special accommodations. We do not craft goods, we do not harvest crops, we do not construct buildings, yet people across the Known Lands shower Historians with charity and kindness. Even the coin we carry is given freely by the Dokkaebi. These offerings are out of reverence for us fulfilling our duty. Should we take actions that warrant remembering, we risk breaking the entire structure upon which our institution is built. What, then, is a Historian if not a recorder of history? So, we must keep our involvement minimal to maintain balance and clarity in our purpose."

Conflict broiled in Aeda. *I've spent my life stuck in Biersport but with a singular purpose, to steal for the Grey Society. Now, I have a chance to do more, and I'm told I should only watch? Why learn all this, then sit back and let the world pass by? I want to do something worth remembering, something worth recording in history.* With the day's events tugging at her eyelids, in a bed of moss with a lattice of branches above, Aeda slipped into a sleep brimming with dreams both comforting and conflicted.

At first Aeda had doubted the sincerity of Iyra's companionship, questioning if the Librarian was merely fulfilling an assignment. As weeks flew by, Aeda came to realize the friendship was quite real and that she had not only gained a mentor in Gieral, but also a friend in Iyra. Though she would have liked to spend more time with them both, she could barely keep up with the barrage of lessons.

Aeda spent what free time she had with Iyra, often venturing into Amrodesa to peruse market shops and watch street performers. Inside the Great Library, Iyra proved an excellent flute instructor. In Aeda's rare moments alone, she communed with Runetrees, scouring the past in the hope she might find a glimpse of her own origins and how she came under the wing of the Grey Society, yet she found not a trace.

One evening Gieral asked Aeda to sit with her in their quarters. "Your instructors are all pleased with your training, Aeda. Tomorrow we will depart."

Leaving so soon and with so little warning. Am I truly ready to be back on the road? Her mind raced, bitter to leave, yet excited for the unpredictable world beyond the city. "Are you certain Delia was pleased?"

"Just because you are not in the library does not mean you cannot learn; I will continue your training. And yes, Delia has been quite happy with your determination and improvement. Cordis is confident you can protect yourself, especially with a spear. You are the first student Bula hasn't complained about incessantly, and Roswalt praises you constantly. Don't fret, we will return to the Great Library soon enough and you will always be welcome to continue training when we visit."

"I didn't think we would leave this soon. I didn't think I would want to stay."

"Well, there's a lesson for you. As a Historian, you must learn to sway in the breeze. We rarely can predict where fate will take us or what events we might witness. We must always be ready for uncertainty. And a few months is like an eternity for Historians. My feet are craving fresh earth beneath them. You should rest; I would like to start early in the morning."

"Where will we be going?"

"Given your previous position as a Thief, I think it fitting for you to learn more about coin. We will head to the Dokkaebi city, Ulburis, the heart of all commerce in the Known Lands."

"But you said Historians are not driven by money. Why would I need to learn about it now?"

"It doesn't hurt to better understand the ebb and flow of life, of which money is a critical part. Besides, the Dokkaebi are a most unique people, and I have a feeling you will appreciate their ways."

"How do you decide where to travel and when to leave?" Aeda questioned, as though the answer might delay their departure.

"At times, Librarians will ask a Historian to visit a place that has not been visited in a while. Occasionally, we decide to travel for a specific purpose, perhaps for a festival or an event. You will be happy to hear that you can choose to visit a city simply because you enjoy being there. Much of the time, I pick a direction and set out, allowing my feet to guide my way."

"Do you think the Dokkaebi have something to do with the disappearing Historians?" Aeda pressed.

"Not in the slightest. Though while we are there, I will speak with a few acquaintances. You should not worry about that matter; I am impressed you even remember I mentioned it amidst the flurry of training. Now, as I said, I would like an early start. It is time for sleep."

Gieral blew out a candle and retired. Aeda's sadness gave way to a joyful anticipation of what new adventure might await. Excitement broiling, she grabbed her flute and left the room. She retreated to a sanctuary, lying under a pale pink Runetree with an arched trunk and drooping brown leaves. She idly played the flute while pondering how different her travels might be as an Apprentice.

A bump on the sole of her foot startled Aeda. Iyra hovered over, giggling, prepared to kick again. "I brought breakfast to your room, but you weren't there, so Gieral and I ate it instead. She said you can eat on your way. But you need to get ready. Gieral has already packed!"

Iyra chatted as they scurried to the Historian chambers. "You must visit as often as you are able. Send letters, tell me where you are going and what you are seeing. I cannot wait to hear of your travels. You must be my eyes outside of Amrodesa! Do you know where you are going first?"

"Ulburis," Aeda replied groggily.

"Ulburis, how wonderful! I envy you in all the places you'll get to see."

"You always talk about seeing faraway places. Why aren't you training to be a Historian instead of a Librarian?"

"I'm happy here. The library is my home, and the Librarians are my family. I can't leave. We're here, you better pack."

"Good morning," greeted Gieral.

"I'm sorry for being late," replied Aeda as warm golden morning light broke into the room.

"Something to remember is that learning never ends. A teacher not only instructs their student, they learn from them as well. And from you, I have found that a morning delay with time for a cup of tea and a bit of reading can be quite refreshing. However, I'm quite done with my book and the tea is cold. Gather your things!"

Aeda hastily filled a bulging hide bag with clothing, books on runewriting, her flute, vials of herbs and seeds, maps, and more. She opened a pouch of coin and stared, transfixed by the glimmering, smooth pieces of gold and silver. *How curious, now an Apprentice Historian and I hold more wealth than I had ever imagined as a Thief.* With a cinch, the purse was closed and tucked into her satchel.

Aeda pulled her tabard on, slung her essence pouches and satchel over opposite shoulders, buckled on her dagger and hatchet, and strung her tome to her belt. Iyra helped hoist on the bulging pack. On the way out, Aeda grabbed a spear Bula had gifted her. The wooden shaft rose above her shoulders and an oiled leather sheath shrouded its leaf-shaped blade.

Few Librarians were awake as the three walked through the Great Library, but the appearance of Roswalt, Delia, Bula, and Cordis in the annex delighted Aeda. They exchanged hugs and words of farewell before the Historian and her Apprentice left, accompanied by Iyra.

While Aeda had been late by Gieral's standards, the residents of Amrodesa were just starting their day. Bakers were furiously kneading floury mounds of dough and butchers' blades sang on whetstones. The merchants Aeda saw brought her back to the morning of the day she met Gieral, a smile breaking as she thought of how different her life was today.

Winding through the city, they arrived at the edge of the river on the outskirts. Moored at the pier was a sailboat, thirty feet long, with a tall mast and vibrant mahogany trim. Loaded with satchels of food and other provisions, only the mildest of ripples radiated out when Aeda tossed in her bag.

"Thank you for everything. I'm not sure how to say goodbye." Aeda took off a bracelet of pale green and white shells strung with fuzzy tan rope, and held it out for the Librarian.

Beaming, Iyra slipped the bracelet on and warmly embraced her friend. "No need to say bye. You will be back soon. I expect to hear all about your travels when you return!"

Aeda waved as Gieral kicked off the pier and unfurled the sail, catching the morning breeze.

CHAPTER

SIXTEEN

The boat cruised swiftly with a sheet full of steady wind. Aeda perched at the bow, dipping a finger in the cool river, leaving gentle wakes behind. The reed-lined banks were home to willow trees with drooping branches that ended in cobalt blue flowers. The sky was full of singing birds and colorful butterflies. Gentle hills cut into farmland until frumpy grasses replaced the fertile fields of grain.

Late in the day, Gieral navigated down a smaller stream. The once smooth hills roughening as dark grey boulders cracked through the earth in rolling mounds of stone. They spent the evening tucked between a rock outcrop and a drooping willow on the riverbank, starting at sunrise again.

At midday they came upon a watchtower with smooth, square-cut stone walls reaching high into the sky. A few Amrodesan guards ran down a slipway until they were knee deep in the river. They waved and held heavy ropes at the ready to moor the boat. Gieral raised a hand to motion the guards away. The men halted, watching bleakly.

"Am I mistaken, or were they expecting us to stop?" Aeda

✦ 146 ✦

asked.

"Yes, they were."

"And… why?" Concern rose in Aeda's voice.

"The sentries are there to keep travelers from venturing too far," Gieral said flatly.

"Venturing too far?" Aeda echoed.

"There is a stretch ahead where rocks close in around the river. There the wind is calm, and the river slows. It is to navigate, and it is usually more expedient to take a different route."

Aeda doubted a tranquil section of water could warrant a watchtower with a garrison. "So, why are we going this way?"

"Before we go to Ulburis, we have a meeting of sorts to attend. It takes place down this bend."

Aeda sulked at the front of the boat. *Not much point in asking more questions. Ever with the cryptic responses. I shouldn't have expected much to change with me as her Apprentice. Gieral is still Gieral.*

The scraggly boulders climbed and formed tall walls around the river. Ages of erosion burrowed curved bends with mocha streaks in sandy grey stone. As they cruised, the space narrowed, leaving only a sliver of sky above. The river's current slowed to a crawl, the sail wrinkling with little more than a light breeze behind it. The monotonous confines tested Aeda's patience, and in the quiet, she missed the bustle of the Great Library.

In what seemed to be the late afternoon, the rock walls widened around a broad section of the river. Aeda imagined the still waters eating the wakes from their boat as hardly a ripple marred the flat and motionless surface. The once-clear river was swirling with murk as if a jar of ink had spilled in. Trees clung to rocks, their roots embedded in crags and branches reaching over the river. Thick moss hung beneath the limbs like curtains, shrouding the quiet stretch in a veil of darkness. A half-rotted pier jutted out from a door-sized scar in the rock wall. Gieral furled the slack sail, winds long calmed and replaced with uncomfortably stagnant and humid air. There was not a sound to be heard other than the splash of oars as she rowed to the decrepit structure.

Nearing the jetty, Gieral joined Aeda at the bow. The sloop bumped into the pier, and it groaned, feeble wrinkles pulsing across the placid river. Gieral secured their craft and dropped a small, hooked anchor, pulling the rope taut against the riverbed. She buckled her sword belt around her waist and stepped cautiously onto the landing, Aeda tiptoeing behind.

The boards flexed and bent under each step, but they held as Gieral rigidly marched along the platform and through the entrance. Aeda delayed in trepidation, not enjoying the thought of entering an unknown cave. A surge of loneliness swelled as she stood in the haunting quiet of the cove, urging her in.

A rush of chilly, musty air greeted Aeda in the darkness. She was relieved to see candles lining the walls in miniature alcoves. The perfectly smooth black domes ended in a point with no visible wick. Instead of flame, it was like a ball of glowing dust was spinning over the candle. Aeda approached one until her nose nearly touched the wall. She jumped at Gieral's voice.

"They are beautiful, aren't they?"

"What are they? They look like candles, but I have seen nothing quite like them."

"They do indeed look like candles, and they give off light

like one, yet that is not their purpose." Gieral's cupped her palm around a swirl of light. She closed her hand, and the illuminated dust slipped between her fingers, returning to their place. "These are remnants of souls, small shreds of a person's innermost being, ripped and bound to these cairns as they released their last breath. A sad reminder of those whose names have been forgotten."

"Was it done with death essences?" Aeda shuddered, aching to leave the hallway lit by the lingering fragments of long-dead souls.

"Yes. As I'm sure Delia told you: rarely, if ever, does any good come from runes written with death essence. These soul cairns are no exception." Gieral drew in a deep breath. "I have the same request for you now as I did with Jakro. Please do not speak a word. While it was important then, it is vastly more important now for you to remain silent during this meeting."

Aeda stiffly nodded her acknowledgement. *Typical. Why be an Apprentice at all if I'm going to be hushed at every turn? I suppose I had better keep quiet this time. Not much good came from letting loose on Jakro.*

They trudged down the hall flanked by soul cairns. At first Aeda tried to count them, but after dozens she lost heart in tallying the reminders of death. Ceasing the mindless exercise, she noticed a wistful melody echoing in the cave. Aeda could not figure what instrument could create such a sound, nor even determine when she first noticed the music.

The path spilled into a domed room with a small passage to the left and a larger one to the right. A snaking crack in the ceiling allowed slivers of light to pour down, illuminating smooth walls. The floor was bare aside from a few splotchy puddles and narrow carvings which led from the walls to the center of the chamber. There, seated on a cylinder of rock, was the source of the music.

A hunchbacked lady was barely visible, the edge of her head peeking over layers of tattered rags on her back. Wisps of long, silvery white hair trailed from her scalp and disappeared beneath the shredded cloth. From behind the tattered hump, the old woman skillfully plucked an unseen instrument.

She turned her head enough for Aeda to see the outline of a pale brow and a gently sloped nose. Her voice was scratchy and brittle, like flaking dried paint. "Hello Gieral, so nice of you to visit. I thought you would be alone, but you have brought company. Shame she isn't a little older."

Aeda realized she had brought only her dagger. *Cordis would not be happy.*

Gieral's lip twitched. "Melinor. The years have been good to you, it seems."

"As good as they have been to you, my dear," snapped the crone, continuing her strumming. "Why did you come here, to my humble home?"

Gieral traced her steps back and forth. "Strange though it may seem, I need your help. I understand it might be difficult for you to think of assisting me, given I am not a wealthy or handsome suitor, but at least it might give you some entertainment. A distraction from your situation, if you will."

"I owe you nothing, Historian, regardless of my wearisome predicament."

"I am sure there is something you desire."

Melinor leaned back and gulped, her throat pulsing and wheezing as she filled her lungs. She spoke with an overbearing sweetness, as if syrup oozed from her lips. "I want a lover, tall, dark hair, plenty of charm, strong features, a heart aching for love and willingness to be wrapped up in my arms. A being who would devote themselves to care and love me to the end of their days. A suitor with deep pockets, enough to satisfy my every whim. But seeing it is just you, I will have to settle for something less, I suppose. I want you to regale me with tales of your latest travels. How I crave to know of the world outside this wretched cave!"

Gieral glared at the diminutive figure in front of her, brow furrowed. Melinor was a deceptive creature, and there had to be some greater cost to the seemingly benign request. Gieral chewed on a piece of candied fruit as she paced behind the old crone's back. The tremors of the music droned incessantly, though Gieral was more concerned with Melinor's words, which clouded and chilled her mind like a heavy fog on a fall morning. The corners of Melinor's mouth twisted and pursed into a grin, her jagged teeth glinting.

"What is wrong my dear, it is a simple request," droned Melinor. "Why don't you share what you need from me?"

"I have a stylus which needs identifying."

"So, take it to an Identifier. That's what they do."

"Jakro had no knowledge of its origin."

"Oh, that is a treat, is it not? I so love it when Identifiers fail, I'm sure Jakro took it well. You have intrigued me, Gieral. I will look at your stylus. What I want in exchange is a pittance."

"There is something more, isn't there?" Gieral said, her voice strained. "You are not one to be easily satisfied, Melinor. You must know you cannot deceive me."

"How could I be a threat to you, the mighty Historian Gieral? I am just an old lady now."

"You are as much 'just' an old lady as I am just a little girl."

"You mean like the one you brought with you?"

Melinor paused her strumming as a clink echoed, the sound of a lock undone. She cackled, her head tilting back in glee. She let out a long, satisfied sigh and resumed her plucking.

"Oh Gieral, you should have known better than to bring a child," gloated Melinor. "It was wise of you to advise her not to speak and sweet of her to obey, but I had no interest in hearing her. Perhaps she should have covered her ears."

"The music, I should have known," Gieral exhaled, metering her words. She spied Aeda slumped by the wall near a lock on the floor. The Historian fought to maintain her poise and resist the dread that was tearing its way up her spine. "One lock of ten, Melinor. Unlocking one does not free the beast."

"Ah yes, the power of a Historian, you can count. Are you so naïve, Gieral? Do you truly believe yourself to be the first to come pay frail old Melinor a visit?" She laughed, her words oozing like venom. "Ten locks from ten jailors, nine undone before today, and on this day, no longer am I shackled!"

Gieral tensed as Melinor shrugged off her rags and cast aside the disguise of a frail old woman with a vigor which betrayed her fragile appearance. Thin silver strands of hair shimmered as she rose. Melinor brought in her ten legs, no longer chained to the ground. They were lengthy, sinewy extensions with many joints, pale and greasy skin drawn taut against her bones like leather on a tanning rack. Clawed toes scraped against the cave floor. Her grotesquely long arms quivered nearly to the ceiling. The music amplified from the fury of her slender fingers, which might seem delicate were it not for their spear-point nails.

Melinor stood for the first time in decades, joints clicking as she moved. Her torso was narrow and elongated as if Ogres squeezed and pulled it. Dozens of distended vertebrae protruded from her back, skin stretched taut between the knobs like a tent canopy pulled between poles. Her ribs bulged from her sides and rattled with each move. The source of her music was finally revealed, innumerable strands of silver hair braided around her spine, each twist, each turn warping the sounds as she plucked.

In a flash, she swung towards Gieral. Her legs mixed with her arms as she cycled her limbs forward, one appendage strumming her stretched hairs while the others would grasp the floor. She now played a discordant cacophony which pained Gieral's ears. Her eyes bulged from a gaunt and wan face as she neared. The Historian stood defiantly, even as Melinor inched forward until their faces were nearly touching.

Through a grotesque smile of unnaturally pearly teeth which stretched nearly to her ears, Melinor giggled. "Oh, my dear Gieral, what a mistake it was to come. What a sweet, delightful, delectable mistake!"

SEVENTEEN

Gieral unsheathed her sword and swung at Melinor's neck with all her strength. The monster flipped back, her torso spinning away as her legs remained balanced around her. Gieral backed down the smaller hallway, blade steady in front.

"How rude to assault your host," Melinor quipped, the smile plastered on her face. "I must admit, it has been ages since I had proper company. Is this how civilized people greet each other now?"

The monster lunged forward with a screech. Her legs spun around the narrow tunnel, outstretched nails flying towards Gieral like talons on a diving eagle. The Historian parried left then right, the edge of her blade deflecting the assault from each hand though Melinor's nails were unscathed. Gieral countered, thrusting her sword at Melinor's throat with a vicious strike, the monster enveloping the steel with her hands and stopping it a breath away from its mark. The Historian heaved but could not free her blade. Melinor kissed the flat of the sword and laughed, sneering while strumming her hair.

"You are an aberration and should never have been allowed to exist!" Gieral roared with fury. She kicked violently against the wall and yanked her sword free. With all her speed and might, she unleashed a flurry of swings, blow after blow; first at a leg, then at an arm, then at the monster's body. The two traced back up the path, dust and rock scattering through the cave.

In the main chamber, the Historian eased her assault, looking to Aeda. Gieral brought in a breath to shout to her unmoving Apprentice, but Melinor countered.

The monster savagely jabbed with her nails. She flipped and twisted, moving with rhythmic steps like a dancer. Gieral retreated down the passage, deflecting and dodging, her steps cadenced by Melinor's music. The incessant battering wore down Gieral. Melinor sensed fatigue and flew into a frenzy, finding success as she clamped her nails down on the sword, freeing one hand to plunge at her prey. Gieral grabbed Melinor's wrist and pushed to deflect the jab, but not enough to prevent a nail from punching through her pauldron and into her shoulder.

Melinor squealed with glee, though Gieral remained stone-faced in defiance. Melinor wrenched the sword and kicked Gieral's legs, forcing her to the cave floor. Poised above, the beast drew back her hand. Over and over, Melinor brought her nails crashing down. Gieral clutched to her sword as she rolled back and forth, shards of stone flying around her.

Melinor grew impatient and heaved Gieral's sword away, the metal clanging as it hit the ground. She pinned the Historian with her now-freed hand, beastly nails raised for a final blow.

Before Melinor could strike, she let out a horrific scream, her wails piercing the halls of the cave. The music ceased, and the air cleared like a stiff wind casting aside fog. She rose to find Aeda, who had fallen behind Melinor, kicking and scrambling away. Back to the wall, she raised her dagger again in a white-knuckle grip as silver strands fell like autumn leaves.

"My hair!" lamented Melinor, boiling with rage. She screeched and lunged for Aeda. "You insufferable rat, I will end you!"

Fear consumed Aeda. She curled her legs to her chest and her hands trembled. Gieral dove for her sword and leapt behind the distracted monster, striking swiftly. She swung left, cleaving a leg. She turned the blade right, severing two more legs. She hewed through an arm and a leg until the sword lodged deep in Melinor's side. The beast shrieked and recoiled as iridescent purple blood ran down her body and spurt from the gash. Her remaining legs gave way and she slipped to the ground, nails scraping the floor inches away from Aeda.

Melinor's legs flailed as she looked back to the Historian, who gripped her sword in place. "Please, Gieral, please don't kill me. Please don't kill me!" she cried, tears falling from fading eyes to join the pooling blood. The Historian pried her blade out of Melinor's side, the writhing monster wailing and grasping at her wounds. Gieral stood tall as blood dripped from her sword.

"How many lives have you taken, Melinor? How many said those very words to you? You are an abomination, and no plea for sympathy or guise of fragility can mask your true nature. Never again will another fall victim to you!"

Melinor hurled herself forward as Gieral brought her sword down with every ounce of might she had. The tip clanged loudly, punching into the cave floor as Melinor's lifeless nails brushed against the edge of Gieral's shirt. The Historian loosed her grip on the sword and sat across from Aeda, who could not tear her gaze away from the suspended monster. She shivered, struggling to sheath her dagger.

"Well, I did not expect to thank you for saving my life a second time, and certainly not this soon," said Gieral, pulling off her damaged pauldron.

"You're hurt. Should I try a healing runeword?" Aeda whispered.

"I will be fine." Gieral wrapped a strip of cloth around her shoulder as calmly as if she were reading a scroll in the Great Library. "Melinor's nails differ from steel. These types of wounds need time more than a rune. How are you? Bodily wounds often heal more predictably than those which affect our mind."

"It was freezing," responded Aeda, still dazed. "It was like I fell into the ocean and the water was filling my head through my ears until I could see nothing but the depths surrounding me. It was terrible."

"I met Melinor once before and have read everything I can find about her since then. Not a single source even hinted at the idea that her power came from music and not words. She was most deceptive to have hidden her skill for this long."

"How was she able to control me with music?"

"Runewriting is not the only way to create runes. It is the easiest and safest method, and therefore the most common. There are also runespeakers, who are exceedingly rare as spoken runes are unwieldy and present great danger to the speaker. And then there are some like Melinor, who are able to craft runes through their music, invisible characters wrought from soul fragments and the air through which the notes pass. Admittedly, I thought there was only one capable of this."

"Who else could create runes like this?"

"Who is not important. Suffice it to know that person is of a kind heart and in a place where they are of no risk to anyone. Let us be thankful that Melinor will no longer be a concern. Come, we should search the chambers. There might be something of interest."

With the bandage tied off, Gieral looked to the corpse. She shook her sword until it came free with a nauseating squelch. Gripping Melinor's nails from the still-attached arm, Gieral swung her blade with a brisk stroke, first severing the fingers with a meaty crunch. Purple droplets splattered against the cave wall.

Aeda's face scrunched in disgust as Gieral repeated the motion with the severed arm and dangled the fingers to let the hewn ends drain. Once the dripping ceased, she rolled them a cloth and tucked the bundle away. She smirked at Aeda's revulsion.

"You, of all people, should understand that value may come in many forms."

The Historian cleaned her sword and returned to the main chamber. Aeda gathered a clump of Melinor's silver hairs from the ground, twisting the strands into a braid which she wrapped around the hilt of her dagger. She took a last look at the unceremoniously abandoned, crumpled corpse. Shivering away a chill, Aeda scurried to the main chamber.

The soul cairns had dissipated with Melinor's death and passing clouds extinguished the scant light from the sky. Aeda could barely make out Gieral's shape, but heard the sounds of rustling. "Hold out your hand. Don't worry, it won't burn, but do not close your hand or the light will go out."

Aeda hesitantly extended her palm while Gieral wrote two glowing orange runewords with flame essences. Aeda marveled as a dense ball of flame hovered a few inches from her hand. She moved her hand up and down, side to side, and in circles, but the light remained in position. Gieral created her own light and led through the larger passageway. They arrived in a spacious den with a low ceiling, complete with tables and chairs, a reading nook, shelves with scrolls and books, chests, and beds. It might have otherwise been a pleasant space, if not for the mummified remains coated in cobwebs that littered the room.

"Nine bodies for the nine locks," Gieral said grimly. "Melinor must have coerced unwary travelers into staying here, likely keeping them alive until she bored of their attention. Have a look around. I will take care of the remains. We may as well spend the night here and get a fresh start in the morning."

Gieral filled the hearth with broken pieces of furniture, igniting the makeshift fuel with the flame in her hand. She carefully arranged the corpses in dignified resting poses, covering each with scraps of tabards and blankets.

Meanwhile, Aeda wavered, not relishing the idea of spending the night in a room with cadavers and Melinor's carcass down the hall. Mustering the confidence to explore, Aeda gave Gieral a wide berth and breezed past stacks of scrolls and books. She pried into containers, pulled open drawers, and perused shelves. Climbing up the side of a tall cabinet stuffed with molding books, Aeda peered over the dusty edge. She was about to end her search when a glint of light caught her eye.

Brushing away webs as opal-shelled spiders scurried away,

Aeda cradled a small metal cube in her palm. The outside was a delicate and ornate lattice of silver ribbons, the strands elegantly twisting and bending. Inside, gears and cogs were packed tightly together. There seemed to be no lock, hinge, handle, or any other discernible way to open the cube.

Gieral had turned her attention from the corpses and was poring over the shelves Aeda had ignored. Sitting down by a neat stack of books close to the hearth, she motioned her Apprentice over.

"What did you find? Bring it here and perhaps I can be more useful than Jakro." Gieral cupped her hand around her Aeda's. "Unlike the Identifier, I believe I will avoid your wrath. I know what this trinket is."

Gieral touched her stylus to her chest and guided a thin stream of sapphire blue soul fragments to the box. Flashes of azure light seared across the surface, and the gears inside spun and whirred wildly. The shell, which Aeda had thought to be a solid piece of metal, opened like a blossoming flower. The delicate constructs within spread, forming a lattice around a tiny yet brightly shining crystal in the center.

"It's beautiful," Aeda whispered.

"You have found a Compass. If you offer it fragments of your soul, it will read your desires and guide you to what you seek. A unique and precious treasure."

Gieral tucked away her stylus and the spinning gears abruptly stopped; the Compass snapping shut in Aeda's hand. She secured the cube under a hidden flap in her satchel.

Too tired to prepare a proper meal, Gieral brought out stuffed loaves of bread and strips of smoked meat. Aeda was reluctant to eat at first, thinking she would have no appetite. A single bite dispelled the notion, as the afternoon's events had instead carved a furious hunger in her. Aeda cleared her mouth with a swig of water and ventured a question.

"Who was Melinor?"

"The story of Melinor is quite a tale," started Gieral. "As far as I'm aware, there are no records of where she came from. All we know is that one day she appeared in Amrodesa. Every morning she would sing by a fountain and play her lute, and crowds would gather to listen. It was said that Melinor's voice was so sweet that the birds would cease chirping when she sang, and she was so beautiful that women would cover their faces when near her for fear of comparison."

"How is it possible we don't know about her past? I thought Historians recorded everything," asked Aeda, laying on a thick straw mat by the crackling fire.

"There are only so many Historians, and our mandate concerns only the history of the Known Lands. She may have come from somewhere far away, perhaps from the desert lands to the north or across the oceans to the west. Historians rarely travel beyond the Known Lands, and much of the history of those places is missing. Perhaps, as powerful as Melinor was, she shrouded herself from recording."

Is it possible I came from those distant lands? Is it possible I have no home at all? "How did she go from singing in Amrodesa to… this?"

"As talented and attractive as she was, many men and women fancied her, and they were happy to give her anything she desired. Some offered all they had and more, and soon enough, she owned quite a stately home in the heart of Amrodesa, elegantly furnished with lavish gifts from her many suitors. Melinor was still unsatisfied, desiring more than material wealth. She abandoned her daily fountain of attention, instead seeking a partner, one who might grant her greater social status. She settled on a handsome and kind bachelor from a modestly wealthy family."

Aeda leaned close, listening with rapt attention as Gieral continued.

"Within a few weeks they were married, the ceremony a jubilant affair with gifts showered on the couple. For a brief while, Melinor basked in the glow of her new and elevated status, constantly pampered and doted on by her husband. In the end, though, the attention of one was insufficient for Melinor. She grew bored with her husband's affection, yet, being a covetous creature, she didn't want someone else to have his love—and certainly not his wealth or status.

"Soon thereafter, her husband announced they would travel across the Known Lands for her enjoyment. Little is known about what transpired on their journey, but not long after, Melinor appeared back in Amrodesa, telling tales of an attack on the road. Eligible again, interest in Melinor was renewed. Many would-be suitors even rode out to find the unknown assailants and avenge her husband's death."

"She must have been lying! Did she kill her husband?"

"Not a single trace of him was found. Melinor, of course, quickly recovered from her grief, returning to the fountain and singing in the streets, the beneficiary of the entire estate of her late husband. Melinor again sought to latch on to a rich and well-respected noble. This time, however, the family was far from thrilled by her presence. The mother took offense and approached Melinor in the streets. Back and forth they screamed. Enraged that someone would dare to challenge her, Melinor shrieked until her bones popped and jutted from her sides. So started her turn into the abomination you saw today."

"How awful! Everyone must have been terrified. She turned into a monster in front of their eyes. What did the people do?"

"People rightly panicked, and the guards chased Melinor from the city. Too ghastly to live near civilization, she settled into a remote cottage. She would entice any who came near with her sweet songs, consuming the souls of those who ventured too close. For countless years Melinor existed that way, a faded whisper, preying on the occasional traveler and binding the remnants of their souls in cairns. With no need to keep up appearances, she allowed herself to decline into the form you saw today."

"But how did she come to be chained in here? Who imprisoned her?"

"Melinor fatefully enticed the younger brother of a renowned warrior. Learning of her sibling's end, the elder sister gathered a company of the strongest and bravest men and women she knew, hell-bent on ending Melinor. They gathered in this very cave, hollowing out the chamber to be her cell. They made a pact in that room, puncturing their ears to prevent her words from taking hold. Eventually they found her cottage, every ledge and table covered in soul cairns. Back then, she was a far more powerful and fearsome creature than she was today, and the battle was said to have lasted for hours, but the brave warriors overpowered Melinor and dragged her to this chamber."

Aeda's interest in Melinor's tale only grew the more she heard. "Why imprison her and not kill her?"

"For all their preparation, for all the rage and hate they carried, not one from the company could bring themselves to destroy Melinor. As for why, that is a question that I do not know the answer to. Perhaps they felt her music even if they couldn't hear her words, which might have been enough. Perhaps it was seeing how sad and broken she was. Given their wrath, perhaps they considered this to be a greater punishment than death. Regardless of the reason, they imprisoned her, to be left alone until she faded from existence."

"But you've seen her before. Others must have known she was here, too. Why did no one else come and kill her if the ones who bound her could not?"

"To execute a bound and helpless creature, at least a seemingly helpless creature, evil though Melinor may have been, is not an honorable act. So, she was a conundrum. Those brave enough and capable of killing her refused because of the dishonor, and those willing were incapable. So here she remained."

"Did you think she had some part in Historians going missing?"

"In short, no. My mentor, from whom I acquired much of my brashness, brought me here many years ago. Unlike him and I, most Historians are wise enough to stay far away from Melinor. I thought, with as much knowledge as she has, or had, perhaps she might have some insight about the owner of the stylus you found. It was a mistake to think that decades of isolation would weaken her."

Aeda lay on her stomach with her head in her hands, mulling over her next words. "You should have told me this before we came here, you know. I'm your Apprentice, and I might have been more helpful if I knew what to expect."

Gieral offered a smile. "You are right. It could only have been beneficial to share. I hope you can accept my apology. You giving her that bit of a haircut was most helpful. I doubt you could have possibly done more to help. Oh, and please don't tell the Head Librarian about this. He might lose his mind if he learns we stopped in to visit old Melinor."

Aeda, used to her thoughts being cast aside by Braedyn, grinned. *Our secret.* She rolled to her side with her back to the fire, head on her satchel while Gieral climbed into one of the creaky beds, both sleeping soundly in Melinor's cave.

EIGHTEEN

They woke early; the fire had long simmered to ash. Gieral insisted on taking a large stack of books and scrolls, Aeda wishing her mentor had found something more like the Compass as she shouldered her share. Extinguished soul cairns lined their way as if they were headstones in Melinor's cemetery. Aeda kept close to Gieral, not wanting to tarry in the presence of the silent graves. She gasped from a blast of crisp morning air. Clouds in the sky flushed pink from the blush of the rising sun.

The river flowed gently around the cave, the muddy water cleared and birds sang in the trees. Aboard the sailboat, Gieral handed a scroll to Aeda.

"Why don't you give that runeword a try," said Gieral, raising the anchor.

Aeda unrolled the scroll, instructions for an air runeword scrawled on the brittle parchment. *This is a complicated runeword.* "Why don't you do it?"

"Because if I do everything, you will be my Apprentice forever. Now give it a go!"

Standing at the rear of the boat, Aeda studied the scroll. She carefully traced the runes, then brought her stylus mindfully through them. To her delight, the sail bloomed and pulled taut from a gust of air.

"Why didn't you cast a runeword like that yesterday, when we were in the narrows?" Aeda smiled, wishing Delia could have seen the full sail.

"I did not know this particular runeword. While I can conjure a breeze, this is far better, a runeword meant precisely for filling sails. I also was in no particular hurry. Now that you have met Melinor, would you have rushed to see her?"

"Not at all."

They emerged from the confines of the rock walls and sailed for two days through open fields of butterscotch grass patched with forests. In the evening, Aeda spied a quaint inn on the shore tucked into a copse of spindly trees. The building hobbled together building showed signs of regular expansion, with colorful rooms branching off each other along the waterfront, adorned by windows of all shapes and beds of charmingly unkempt flowers. Aeda found the sign particularly delightful, portraying the face of a hog with a wool-covered body. Painted gold words proudly announced it as The Sheepish Pig Inn. She was thankful when Gieral furled the sail and eased towards the tavern.

A girl in coarse trousers with auburn hair ran out onto a pier, helping tie off the boat to a bollard. The Historian and her Apprentice gathered their bags, the girl ushering them through an oddly wide door and into the inn. Inside was an inviting room with aged wooden walls and creaky floorboards. Splotchy paintings on the walls—all of which included at least one pig and one sheep—humored Aeda. She leaned, tilting her head for closer inspection. It became clear many of the sheep and pigs were later additions, painted with less-trained hands than those of the original artists.

Seated at a long table in the center of the room was a diverse group of patrons: Humans, Bog Elves, Sea Nymphs, Spriggans, and one particularly tall Dokkaebi. They were noshing on stewed vegetables, tender braised meat and smashed potatoes in a pool of herb gravy on pewter plates. The innkeeper was a jovial man with an extraordinarily red beard who greeted the two warmly.

"Welcome, welcome! So pleased to see a Historian and her young Apprentice! Please, have a seat and we'll get you a plate. Don't you dare pull out that pouch, all Historians eat free at the Sheepish Pig!"

Not a Thief, something more, something respectable. Aeda knew she would forever remember the Sheepish Pig Inn as the first place that someone recognized her as a Historian.

Aeda tore into the communal meal, hot food especially delicious after days spent bobbing on the river. Her stomach filled to its capacity, she almost nodded off when the door burst open. A tall man shrouded in a bulky cloak filled the entryway. Taking a large step forward, he smacked his head on the door frame and fell to his rear. The onlookers broke into laughter as the man acrobatically leapt up to his feet and cast off his cloak, revealing a row of pipes on a frame beneath his chin, a drum on his back with strings tied to his shoes, and a lute tucked under his arm. Cheers burst out as the troubadour danced, strummed, blew, and cavorted around the room.

Gieral grabbed their bags and slipped away to their room.

On returning, she found Aeda stomping on a table with the bard as revelers clapped and danced along. Gieral slid into a comfy chair in the corner, finding her own joy in a clay mug of stiff mead. For hours and hours, past the setting of the sun and into the dark of the early morning, she watched Aeda sing and dance and rejoice. The party carried on until the jester himself collapsed asleep on the table, and Gieral hauled Aeda to bed.

Gieral woke her snoring Apprentice with a shake, the girl half-hanging off her bed. Craning her neck, Aeda saw a smidge of orange on the horizon through the window. She let her head drop freely back to her pillow.

"Are you quite certain it's the right time for me to be awake? Why don't you pour yourself a cup of tea? We have all those scrolls from Melinor's cave," she groaned in a hoarse, futile protest.

"The day has already begun, and the road is awaiting our feet," chided Gieral.

"Why do you go to caves when you could spend more time in places like this?" Aeda rolled over, reluctant to leave the cozy bed.

"The festivities last night were quite enjoyable, but remember what I told you of overstaying. We spent the night on the charity of the innkeeper, and our presence does not bring any value to him. We are observers, not doers, and to stay and revel in the generosity of our hosts would be a disservice to their kindness."

Aeda finally dragged herself up. "Why don't we help them out to make ourselves more welcome?"

Gieral yanked away Aeda's blanket with a grin. "Enough procrastinating, out of the bed! You may as well have been a market crier, jabbering yourself awake. I understand your meaning, but as Historians we drift with the ebb and flow of the tide, we do not build piers on the beach. Our purpose is to record history, and intentionally delaying your travels for the sake of a comfortable bed would not be appropriate."

Aeda rubbed the sleep away from her eyes as she cinched down her belt. *Once I'm a Historian on my own, I'm going to do something of note, big or small no matter, but I will do something, somewhere, to be remembered and welcomed upon my return.* Pack shouldered and spear in hand, Aeda followed her mentor out. The morning was cool, prompting her to snug a bulky scarf around her neck and pull her cloak over her shoulders.

A vacancy at the pier startled Aeda. "We're not taking the boat?"

"No," replied Gieral. "While you were sleeping, I arranged for it to be taken back to Amrodesa. We will walk the rest of the way to Ulburis."

Gieral preempted questions about breakfast and handed Aeda a parcel wrapped in crinkling paper. Inside was a loaf of sweet bread with neatly layered ribbons of spiced onion, squash, and sausage. Contentedly munching, she followed her mentor onward to the Dokkaebi city.

They eased through the day, the scrappy hills of tall green and tan grass fading into a gentle field with burnt orange clay streaks speckled with pods of twisted grey trees with drooping olive leaves. That evening, Aeda felt at home in their camp, listening to embers crackle as she gazed at the stars and moons above.

The next day, the path narrowed in an increasingly harsh landscape. Hills rose and fell, and boar-sized sepia stones broke through the earth. Near midday, fog set in and blurred the sun, Aeda barely able to see Gieral ahead. Frustrated with the rigorous trek, she cried out between heavy breaths. "If Ulburis is the center of all commerce, then surely there is an easier way to get there."

"Yes," Gieral cheerily responded. "In fact, there are many well-paved roads leading Ulburis, no doubt crowded with travelers hauling carts laden with goods."

"Then why are we taking this trail if there are better roads?"

"Not necessarily better roads. Undoubtedly easier, but easy does not always mean better. Tell me, when you were a Thief, did you learn more about thieving from easy marks or difficult ones?"

"Of course, the difficult ones," Aeda groaned, knowing the lesson that would follow.

"Then you know that the challenging path is the one that offers the greatest potential for us to grow. I prefer these paths because they are far more exciting than roads traveled by multitudes of people every day. If you see something interesting on a well-traveled road, then you are one of many to see the interesting thing. In fact, it may not be interesting at all. Now imagine something catching your eye on a path such as this."

"I don't think I'll see much through this fog," Aeda sassed.

"Perhaps this moment is not the best example, but on less traveled roads, anything notable might be something that no other person will ever experience. And that is why we will often take these routes, difficult though they may be. Besides, this path is not a terrible one."

They scrambled over a tortuous, crumbling trail for a seemingly endless time. Aeda was relieved when Gieral finally halted, the fog as dense as a storm cloud. Aeda prepared to query the reason for the pause, but sighed in awe when a gentle breeze cleared the view.

A distant rumble filled Aeda's ears as she took in the sight of a steep hill before them, leading to an open plain surrounded on three sides by rocky cliffs. Stalls in neatly ordered rows formed the most immense marketplace she had ever seen, far larger than all the markets in Biersport combined. They were too numerous to count, each with a flamboyantly colored canopy; some rose to high points, others gently tapered, adorned with stripes, crests, ruffles and tassels.

"There are times," said Gieral mischievously, "when the most interesting path is also the easiest."

She gently slid the tip of her sword into the middle of a broad and flat rock. Wiggling the blade, she separated a seat-sized slab which thundered to the ground. She separated a second in the same way, then lashed a rope around the front of each stone. Gieral pushed the slabs to the edge of the hill and sat on one, taking the cord in hand.

"Well, come on then," invited Gieral.

I've thought she's mad before, but she must be joking. "Surely you're joking."

"Not in the slightest, now sit, or we will have to camp up here for the night."

Under her mentor's stare, Aeda warily sat on the slab. Gieral shoved the back of Aeda's stone. Aeda screamed as she hurtled down the slope, bits of rock crumbling beneath her unwieldy ride. Her yells soon changed to cries of joy as she tacked the stone back and forth. Gieral zoomed by, leaving a wake of dust and tumbling stone. The Historian deftly leapt off the stone as the hill leveled into the valley. Aeda rolled off the stone slab as it caught on a stump, laughing as Gieral pulled her upright.

She brushed at the clay, but forgot the dust when she looked up to see the market a stone's throw away. Behind each booth was a Dokkaebi, furiously haggling and negotiating with customers, none of whom were Dokkaebi. Merchants from across the Known Lands milled about the stalls, coins flowing like rice in a granary. Aeda recognized some merchants from Biersport by their clothing, a small sample in a range and breadth of appearances that overwhelmed her eyes. At every turn was a curious face, a Spriggan whose long beard looked like hanging lichens, a woman with a bright pink fez, a Bog Elf with a flowing green robe.

Gieral patted Aeda's back, leaning away from a puff of dust. "Welcome to the Overmarket of Ulburis."

"If this is the market, where is the city?" inquired Aeda, straining over the boisterous scene.

Gieral leaned in, speaking just shy of a yell. "The city itself is underground. In fact, this is one of two markets. The Overmarket is for traders to come and exchange goods, hoping to make a fortune selling their wares to the Dokkaebi. It can, however, be difficult to predict what the Dokkaebi might want. I once saw a man bring family heirlooms, generations old pottery, masterfully crafted, which were completely unwanted. In his despair, he cracked his stylus over his knee. A passing Dokkaebi offered him three fingers of gold for it."

"Why would a Dokkaebi pay that much for garbage?"

"Dokkaebi are collectors. They have built their entire society on trading, negotiating, and haggling to assemble collections of whatever they fancy. They often seek items of a particular theme. That Dokkaebi was searching for items which were damaged by their owners in moments of desperate rage. The stylus that the young man broke happened to fit perfectly."

Aeda was utterly astounded as they wandered through the heart of the Overmarket. Constant sounds and sights competed for her attention as Dokkaebi and merchants alike offered goods of all kinds. Two Dokkaebi competed for a spool of thread. A fork with three bent tines was hastily exchanged for a bulging pouch. Meanwhile, a necklace encrusted with jewels brought not even a sliver of excitement from the Dokkaebi.

The entrance to Ulburis waited at the end of the market, carved into a sheer face of rock. Two dust-coated doors, each about twice the width and twice the height of a normal door, sealed the city. They were an oddly dull backdrop to the vibrant market, not the auspicious entryway Aeda had expected. Gieral tugged a giant bronze ring hanging from a door, striding confidently into the shadowed recess.

Aeda cursed the worthlessness of two low-burning torches placed far too high on the walls. A bang sounded from behind and she clutched her spear, spinning to find Gieral had shut the door. The Historian shrugged, Aeda hoping the dark masked her flushed cheeks.

Opposite the doors was a square panel of wood, painted bright yellow and easily twenty feet wide. Flanking the panel were pale, almost ghostly statues of Ogres grasping giant bronze hooks. Aeda felt quite uneasy in their presence, remembering the footsteps of the Ogre in the Dokkaebi caravan. Gieral cleared her throat and patted one of the Ogre's hands.

Aeda jumped, her spear dropping to the floor with a clang as the Ogres, quite alive, grumbled and stretched. The Ogres inserted their hooks in sockets on each side. They twisted them like keys and the panel separated into four triangular sections. In sequence, the bottom quarter folded down, the top quarter raised, then the left and right quarters pivoted aside, revealing a passage with smooth rock walls. Aeda scooped up her spear and hurried after her mentor. *At least Cordis wasn't here to witness this.*

"Why do there always seem to be Ogres with the Dokkaebi?" Aeda asked as they strolled down the wide hall.

"Ogres are simple creatures. They aren't stupid, but they thrive when given clear duties. Meanwhile, mining ore and forging coins are arduous tasks and the Dokkaebi are quite grateful for their assistance. So, in the end, Ogres have fulfilling work and the Dokkaebi benefit from their strength. Remind me to tell you about the Ogre uprising sometime and you will understand why the entirety of the Known Lands is grateful for this relationship. Anyhow, an altercation with an Ogre should be the least of your concerns.

"As for the Dokkaebi, they have a unique, almost fanatical appreciation for clever trading. For example, if one Dokkaebi swindles another, they would garner great respect from the victim for their cleverness, particularly if the sham was creative or unexpected."

"I wish I was born a Dokkaebi," Aeda said wistfully,

imagining her assortment of pilfered oddities on display in the Overmarket.

"Our lives are, in some ways, like seafaring ships," consoled Gieral. "We don't choose what port we start in, but once at sea, it is up to us to navigate ourselves to the destination of our desire. It may not have been your choice to start life in Biersport as a Thief, and perhaps you would have been happier as a Dokkaebi, but we are not afforded the luxury of selecting our origin. What matters more is the choices we make, such as you embarking on this journey to become a Historian."

"Can't we change where we call home?"

"Home is an interesting concept. In truth, for most Historians, the Great Library is the closest thing we have to a true home. Yet regardless of where you refer to as home today, you cannot change where you started. You will always have your past in Biersport, the same way my life on the Moor shaped me. Even if you no longer call that place home, even if it is a place you don't remember fondly, it will always be a part of you and it is your choice what you do with that experience. For Historians, whose journeys are as important as their destinations, it is especially important, as your origin sets the stage for the story of your life."

Aeda then knew what she would use for her stylus. In the bottom of her satchel was a slender wooden handle from a ship's steering wheel, removed while stealing from the captain. It was smooth from the sea, with two thin brass rings and a monkey's fist knot carved at the end. She tucked it in her belt, a permanent reminder of how she would grow beyond her past in Biersport.

At the end of the passage was a plaza more than a hundred

feet across, with tiled floors and dozens of open doorways. Gieral selected one, and they entered a room broad enough to comfortably fit a dozen people. Metal pillars joined with wire mesh rose like a cage. There were no furnishings except for a single lever jutting out from the back wall, a dented and tarnished bar with a handle wrapped in fabric that might have once been bright red. Aeda looked at her mentor, confused by the odd space.

"Go ahead, give it a pull," encouraged Gieral.

Aeda yanked the lever with a drop of her shoulders. At first, the only noticeable effect was a soft whistle. She leaned in to examine the lever when the world gave out from beneath her.

Aeda gulped, her hair flipping up from the free fall. Fear turned to wonder as the descent slowed down blackened steel tracks, revealing a cavern more immense than she could ever have imagined.

The cave could have easily fit the entirety of Biersport, the ceiling seemingly as high as the trees of Amrodesa were tall. Broad flows of magma ran along the boundaries, imparting a pleasant warmth and a distinctive mineral odor. Ulburis had three districts, joined around a pillar many times larger than Namuor. Nearest was an immense market. To the right was a banquet hall with thousands of dwellings on its perimeter, and to the left was the mint, an expansive smithy fueled by lava bubbling through open seams. The cavern glowed from clusters of fluorescent mosses and mushrooms, burning torches, flickering lanterns, and the oozing magma.

The elevator jerked to a stop and Aeda burst forward, bounding over a rock floor carved to look like cobblestones.

Passing a few idle Dokkaebi, she leaned on a ledge overlooking the city.

The bazaar was as vast as the Overmarket, full of stalls where Dokkaebi presented their wares with speeches and declarations and flailing arms. Many Dokkaebi roamed the aisles toting small bags and hauling bulging satchels, some even pulling carts. Curiously, not a single coin was in sight.

"Welcome to the Market," Gieral said.

"No special name?" Asked Aeda.

"It doesn't need a special name, as it is the market of all markets, and its name reflects that."

"If it is the market of all markets, then why is there no money?"

Gieral chuckled, sharing a piece of candied fruit. "These are questions you should ask of the Dokkaebi themselves. Come, let us make our way to the forges, and there your questions will be answered."

Gently sloping stairways spread from each side of the platform to the Market. Treading down steps worn smooth from ages of use, they arrived at the edge of the Market. The Dokkaebi were in a frenzy, their faces painted in every emotion from humored delight to vitriolic ire.

Gieral and Aeda stayed on the outskirts of the Market. Another set of sprawling stairs brought them to the mint. A chunky Dokkaebi, wearing a faded cinnamon shirt with blue trousers, sat with his arms crossed over his belly. His blackened goggles slouched above his brow, corralling shocks of wiry and unkempt white hair. Upon noticing Gieral, he sidled over until his belly brushed against her buckle. Squinting, he let out a loud "humph" and spat off to the side.

Gieral spoke flatly. "You're balding spectacularly, Taphes. And you have gotten quite portly as well."

The Dokkaebi burst into laughter, cheerfully punching Aeda's shoulder. "Always good to see you, Gieral. And who is this?"

"My Apprentice, Aeda," replied Gieral.

"You? An Apprentice? I heard you say *your* Apprentice, yes? Not someone else's on loan? How'd that come to be?"

"She was formerly a Thief in Biersport and stole from me. To make an exceptionally long story short, she proved to be more than worthy of the position."

"Ha! I'll have to hear the long version someday. I couldn't imagine a better Apprentice for you than a Thief."

"Emphasis on *former* Thief. I was hoping you might have a bit of time to teach her about the Dokkaebi, particularly the economic side of things."

Taphes smiled, pointed teeth on display. "Shirking your duties already, Gieral, eh? Asking someone else to lecture your learner. Most interesting, your Apprentice. In any case, a *former* Thief is certain to do well among us. She should have the right wiles to navigate Ulburis. It will take a few days to cover everything. I can't skip over our culture in favor of coin. You know, it is all mingled."

"The short version, Taphes," replied Gieral. "I have business with the caravans. Make sure he stays out of trouble, won't you, Aeda?"

Gieral took Aeda's pack and spear and left her with Taphes. The Dokkaebi hopped onto a barrel coated in grease and soot. "I don't know what Gieral has told you, but I'm sure you have plenty of questions. Not many better ways to learn than to ask and be answered."

"Gieral called the Ulburis Market the market of all markets. Why is there no money?" Aeda asked excitedly, relieved at how eager he was to answer compared to Gieral's typically compulsory responses.

"To answer that question, we must examine the nature of the Dokkaebi," began Taphes. "First off, in the Dokkaebi society, we share many aspects of our life. All Dokkaebi live in similar homes and we all eat the same meals, communally, in the banquet hall."

"I don't mean to be rude," Aeda interjected, "but Gieral told me about Dokkaebi collections, and I thought you all would be a bit more... individual."

"Food is sustenance, and a dwelling is a place to sleep. Those are necessities. Just because we share the basics of existence does not mean we are all the same. What matter is it if the mundane is common among all? Finding items to grow our collections, that is where Dokkaebi derive joy and happiness.

"You see, for us, coins are uninteresting because there is nothing distinct about coins, nothing to separate one nail from another. Simply, coins are dull. Above-grounders like to judge and value each other based on ownership of coin. Us Dokkaebi, we ask, why should we measure ourselves with the same bits of metal? There's nothing individual about that at all! So, we are fiercely proud of our collections, trading and haggling with material goods and never with money."

Aeda could hardly imagine living surrounded by wealth but never using it. "I thought Dokkaebi were the masters of coin?"

"We Dokkaebi have been entrusted with the sole right and claim to make coins of any kind. It's our duty to manage currency, much like a Historian's duty is to record history. All the gold, silver, and copper nails and fingers in the Known Lands are made in the image of our hands, a reminder of our purpose."

"So, the people who don't care about coins are the stewards of it?"

"Precisely. Our disinterest in coins are what make us such good managers of it. No threat of theft if we don't want what is up for grabs."

"Then the Dokkaebi have a never-ending supply of money? Is every Dokkaebi rich?" Aeda found it difficult to shake a covetous desire for such wealth.

"Ha!" Taphes snorted, tickled by the question. "Yes, every Dokkaebi is rich, but not in the way you are thinking. I told you we don't care for coins. We are richly satisfied by the lives we lead."

"But what about all the coins I saw in the Overmarket?"

Taphes hopped down from the barrel and walked along the edge of the mint, the magma radiating an uncomfortable warmth. "Look, see these carts?

Aeda peeked over the ledge. On shiny metal tracks were black carts nearly as large as the Ogres pulling them.

"Inside those bins are pouches of sorted nails and fingers. Any Dokkaebi wishing to join the Overmarket may nab one on their way out, providing them with currency to trade with. When they come in at the end of the day, they simply dump whatever remaining coins they have down a collection flue, and they are on their way. In the meantime, our Ogre friends grab the bags for counting and reconciliation."

"One market can't possibly be the only way to distribute coins," Aeda replied dubiously. "I saw a group of Dokkaebi and an Ogre pulling a cart near Hrold's Hand."

"Correct! The Overmarket is but one piece of the puzzle, though it might surprise you to know how much coin flows there. In reality, much of the balancing comes from the caravans. Based on our accounting, we send caravans to cities and towns, some taking coins, others retrieving it."

"Why would the cities let the Dokkaebi caravans take money from their coffers? What if they refuse?"

Taphes grinned impishly. "It is time for a Dokkaebi to teach the Historian's Apprentice a small lesson about the power of the mandates which we abide by. The responsibilities of the Dokkaebi are recorded as far back as history goes in Runetrees. They are so well defined and intertwined in the threads of life, to defy them is to run against the laws of existence in the Known Lands. If any one city or town refused, then every resident of the Known Lands would be bound to address the offending group. Duty to react aside, it's an economical unfairness that no one would take lightly. Angering all the cities at once is not a pleasant proposition."

Taphes brought Aeda to a giant stalagmite with a round metal door cut into the side. He turned a small brass key in an unremarkable iron lock and the door rolled aside. Clanging and banging greeted them, and long sheets of unbound inky paper streamed through the air. The room was as large as the Runewriting Hall in the Great Library. Dozens of u-shaped machines filled with pulsing silver runes flanked the walls. Inside each sat a Dokkaebi, hammering furiously at buttons and pulling levers as they reviewed the scribbled ledgers. Gears whirred and the machines spewed printed paper sheets which Dokkaebi scampered to collect and review.

"Here is where the accounting occurs. Our caravans bring ledgers, records of their disbursals and collections, along with insights on the economic clime of different regions. We count the coins from the Overmarket, combine it with the caravan information, then our calculators go to work. These are the fine Dokkaebi who decide when to send out caravans, how much to send to the Overmarket, and the like."

"Impossible," Aeda murmured in disbelief that the chaotic assembly of Dokkaebi managed such a precise and calculated matter of importance.

"I assure you, this isn't a cover for a more elegant and sophisticated system. Countless generations of practice and learning can do wonders. Besides, if we make a mistake, we will realize it in short order and rectify the error in a day or two, not as if anyone would know except us!" Taphes said with a wink.

He chuckled as they left the busy Dokkaebi to their work, and leaned against a stalagmite while Aeda surveyed the rest of the mint.

The district ended in a passage from which Ogres hauled laden slings. They emptied sorted chunks of ore into three enormous vats, larger than sailboats, that were heated by magma furnaces. Streams of molten metal oozed from the vats into channels which fed Dokkaebi-sized pots. Once full, they tipped, pouring into finger-shaped molds where Ogres stamped presses to shape the metal.

The Ogres piled the freshly pressed coins on tables where Dokkaebi stacked and wrote counts on smudged paper. A short distance away, Dokkaebi sorted through bins of returning fingers and nails, tossing damaged coins to be melted down and grouping acceptable ones to join those freshly minted. Aeda stared agape at the endless sea of coins. *One table must hold more wealth than the entirety of Biersport! How perfect the stacks look, untouched, unclaimed, unburdened by the expectation of something in return.*

"Now you're a right authority on Dokkaebi I'm sure. Any more questions?"

Aeda gratefully accepted a rag from Taphes and wiped her brow. "If the Dokkaebi love the markets and trading that much, how do you choose who has to run the mint?"

"It would be nice if we could spend every day gallivanting about the Market, yes, but we can't exactly eat our collections nor does trading in the Market fulfill our mandate. Each Dokkaebi must spend at least half their time working, whether at the forges, in the counting house, in the mines, out with a caravan, building and repairing, or harvesting food. And if a Dokkaebi tries to avoid their responsibility, it becomes quite apparent. We have no time for greediness with our work. That is saved for the markets."

"What about the Dokkaebi I've seen above ground? I mean outside the Overmarket, like at Amrodesa? What's to stop a Dokkaebi from taking a mass of coins and traveling across the Known Lands?"

"No need to be subversive. We welcome travel! In fact, that is how I met Gieral, a chance encounter in Amrodesa many years ago. If a Dokkaebi wants to travel above ground, they take with them precisely the average amount of wealth carried by visitors to their first planned destination. That way, they are on an even footing and won't upset the flow of coin, but they're also in a good enough position to enjoy their travels and bring back interesting items for trade.

"Now you have spent a fair bit of time listening to me. You should explore Ulburis! If you have more questions, you'll probably find me somewhere around the mint. I'm stocking up on workdays at the moment so I can enjoy a lovely stretch of trading. If you were to ask my opinion, I would advise you to experience the Market. Nothing in the Known Lands quite like it. You have a few hours before it closes." Aeda was prepared to rush off, but Taphes reined her in. "Ah, tarry a moment. Let me share a few more morsels of advice to chew on. I'm a believer in learning through experience, but Gieral will be cross if I don't caution you properly.

"First, nothing is more sacred to a Dokkaebi than a trade. Once a trade is made, it is absolutely final. Second, never trade your time. Time seems cheap when you are young, but trading time is dangerous. It is a seemingly easy way to gain what you want, but is easily advantage of. And third, assume that every

Dokkaebi is trying to swindle you. Because they are. There is no such thing as charity in the Market, not even for a Historian."

"That seems rather harsh?"

"It's not mean spirited, we're just a little zealous. You're new, so be mindful. We almost never get visitors down here other than the occasional Historian, which means Dokkaebi won't think to treat guests in the Market any different. If that's all, off you go then, I'm sure Gieral will find you when you're needed."

Aeda graciously thanked Taphes, then made her way briskly through the city. It was a strange sensation to be alone, her time spent roaming Biersport a hazy memory. At the Market, she found the Dokkaebi jumping and yelling, sprinting from stall to stall. Aeda chewed at her lip, wondering how she was supposed to join.

Casting aside her trepidation, she took a deep breath and stepped in. Aeda expected to be singled out, but she instead found herself largely ignored. She neared a stall with a plump, sour-faced Dokkaebi sitting behind rows of colorful little glass jars, topped with painted corks which shimmered with runes.

"Come right over, little girl," he pantomimed as if he were a circus ringmaster. "My name is Mato. I am sure you'll want to see my wares, all contents kept fresh under the seal of runes. Ah, how convenient, you are a runewriter. You can check the runes yourself for authenticity!"

Aeda picked up a tall, thin jar and peered in at the viscous, chunky liquid inside. Though thoroughly disgusted, she did not want to be rude to the proud Dokkaebi. "What… what is inside the jars, and why might I want one?"

The Dokkaebi smiled gleefully and hovered over his wares.

"I, Mato, am the dealer of the finest bodily fluids in the Market, contained and preserved with the most meticulous set of runes. In your hand is a sample of vomit from the current Head Librarian, collected when he was still a young boy. A good year indeed."

Aeda stifled a gag, stiffly placing the jar back on the table. "Why would I want a jar of bodily fluids?"

"You look to be a Historian in training. I am not the one to know what you're collecting. Librarians, Historians, you lot are always working together. Well, if Librarians are not it, I have this jar of Historian's urine, nearly two hundred years old. It could be perfect!" He lifted a stout jar and shoved it inches from Aeda's face, the contents sloshing unsettlingly against the cork seal. "For you, young Historian, I will make an exception and go easy on the trade."

A few passing Dokkaebi laughed as Aeda unsuccessfully attempted to repress a dry heave. She politely declined, and Mato laughed jovially and turned to another Dokkaebi.

Continuing down the rows, the array of goods enthralled Aeda. Some Dokkaebi pushed uniform and polished collections, like a stall decorated with dozens of pristine helmets. Other stalls had such a diverse and indistinguishable mixture it was impossible to guess what the unifying factor might be, such as one Dokkaebi with a motley array of tree bark, shoe soles, coiled instrument strings, and chairs, each with one broken leg.

The constant glow of the cavern made time pass strangely, intensified by Aeda's interest in everything she saw. Eventually Gieral came into view, sidling through the crowd to greet her Apprentice. *How long have I been here? It feels like only minutes have passed!*

"I see you finished with Taphes. Did he caution you about trading in the Market, or did he just set you loose?"

"He told me not to wager my time and to assume every Dokkaebi was trying to cheat me."

"Not inaccurate. Though I wonder, did he remember to mention any of the formalities of the Market?"

"Formalities?"

"Where to begin. Each year, we elect three Dokkaebi to become the new Officiants. It is their responsibility to open and close the Market each day until the next election." Gieral pointed to a platform cut into the side of the stalagmite at the heart of Ulburis. It was large enough for a dozen people to stand comfortably, with a commanding view of the Market. "In the morning, they proceed to the dais. One Officiant opens the charter, which is the record book of Ulburis. The second Officiant, carrying an official stylus, writes in the date and notes the opening. The third Officiant recites what was written, and the trades may begin both here in the Market and in the Overmarket above. They repeat the process to close at the end of the day."

"That sounds formal for the Dokkaebi. Everything else seems relaxed."

"It is mostly symbolic, though in symbols there is great power and meaning, as evidenced by runes."

"Does anything else get written in the charter?"

"It is exceptionally rare for something else to be added. Many of the tendencies and expectations of Dokkaebi, such as working and not only trading, are in the early pages. Part of the reason for the infrequency is that if a new idea is written in, a majority of the Dokkaebi in the Market must vocalize their agreement for it to take on any meaning, even if the Officiant has read it from the charter. You try getting an entire city that is either eager to trade or weary and ready for a meal to agree on a topic. Further, this way of life quite satisfies the Dokkaebi, and the few who are unsatisfied usually live above ground."

"Can we meet the Officiants?" Aeda asked.

"Perhaps we can catch them at breakfast."

"Why not at dinner?"

Gieral grinned and placed a hand on Aeda's shoulder. "Come then, the Market is closing soon. We can intercept them and see if they are open to sharing a meal."

TWENTY

The Officiants appeared on the dais overlooking the Market, standing auspiciously in the center. Wispy, speckled grey hair grew like dried grass from cracked stones in a street. Their silken robes shimmered with patterns of gold and silver thread, distinguishable from each other by bands of colored trim.

The first Officiant, in a pale lavender robe, lifted a fist-sized orb out of her pocket by a chain. Orange runes pulsed as if caged in the glass, with two black metal spheres lazily flowing around the exterior. The two spheres snapped together at the top of the orb and it instantly turned teal. The Dokkaebi nodded to her peers.

They stepped to the edge of the dais, and activity in the Market ceased. The cavern was eerily quiet, absent all sound save the distant echoes of Ogres working forges. An Officiant adorned in summery green cracked open the tome. Their compatriot, dressed in tangerine orange, made a great show of scrawling a few tiny words on the open page. In turn, the Officiant in purple glanced at the writing and sputtered, "Market is closed on this day."

A murmur of reluctance took over the cavern. Dokkaebi threw cloths over their stalls and stowed away their belongings before filing towards the communal hall for dinner.

Gieral and Aeda awaited the Officiants at the bottom of the dais, the three mumbling a collective greeting on seeing the Historian.

"Good evening Domeri, Arhal, Kalem. May we join you for dinner?"

Kalem grumpily pulled at the sleeve of her lavender robe. "We? It has only ever been you, Gieral. Other Historians are respectful enough to leave us Officiants alone."

"This is my Apprentice, Aeda. She asked if it might be possible to dine with you."

Aeda bowed, Kalem merely squinting in response.

"I suppose," Domeri droned, his green robe scrunched unevenly across his shoulders.

"They would probably weasel their way in regardless of your answer," said Kalem, dourly.

"Dinner would not be too much trouble," closed Arhal, pulling an orange sash tight across his waist.

The Officiants scurried away, chattering amongst themselves with slurred and smeared words as if the mere idea of enunciation was offensive. Aeda was furiously hungry and trotted behind the Officiants at the tail of the amorphous flow of Dokkaebi headed to supper. As grand as the two markets were, she was brimming with anticipation of what exciting food might be served.

Unlike the orderly rows of market stalls, the banquet hall was a chaotic mess. Dokkaebi flocked around mismatched tables, which were scattered without reason. Carrying on the spirit of the Market, Dokkaebi clambered over each other, vying for seats as if taking part in a city-wide game of musical chairs. The Officiants groaned, settling on an uneven round table with five seats at the fringe of the hall. By the time the group sat, most of the Dokkaebi were already served and the banquet hall was a chorus of slurping and chewing.

Waiters unceremoniously tossed a platter with flatbread into the center of the table and set a bowl for each diner. The muted light of the cavern made it difficult to discern the contents, though what Aeda could make out seemed less than inviting. Chunky globs clung to the bowl as she lifted her first spoonful with a *shlop*. Aeda took a hesitant bite, finding the taste modestly better than the looks. The mixture was earthy with tender meat and plump mushrooms, though it lacked spice and seasoning.

"It is good you enjoy the food, meager though it may be," moped Arhal. "Most visitors don't seem too keen on trying our humble fare."

"Gieral never seems to have a problem, would not expect her Apprentice to be any different," said Kalem grouchily.

"Why wouldn't visitors want to eat your food?" asked Aeda, chewing on a giant mouthful, her hunger eclipsing any distaste.

"You are eating a stew of ground moss, fermented fungus, boiled mushrooms, and pickled lizard meat," shared Gieral softly between strained bites.

Aeda choked at the description, a gelatinous mouthful dripping down her chin. The Officiants broke into laughter, joined by Gieral. Aeda wiped her face and grabbed a piece of bread. "Since you're in the Market all day, you must be able to trade to your heart's content. If you don't mind me asking, what do you all collect? Is there something particular you are trying to acquire?"

Kalem's nostrils flared. "We hardly have time to trade. We start the Market; we close the Market. Then, in between, it is our responsibility to help resolve disagreements, no matter how trivial. We're tied down all day, no time to even think about going to the Overmarket. And I tell you sure as a Spriggan loves trees that most of these requests for arbitration are falsehoods done simply to prevent us from trading."

Domeri continued dryly. "Even in the time we can trade, because of our position, everyone is fickle with us. They are ridiculously unreasonable with their expectations of a trade, many demand something from the Overmarket and they know we can't make our way there."

Arhal clarified dispassionately. "When Dokkaebi trade, there is much more involved than the objects themselves. Who you are trading with, whether the items broaden your collection or enable a trade for an item you desire, how the items were acquired, and what the stories are behind them, especially the stories, all change the value of items. It is hard for us to bring items for trade with good stories owing to our demanding duties as Officiants.

"Now, to answer your question, I have taken it on myself to acquire items of pivotal importance that affected the course of history. What I most desire for my collection is a golden spoon. Not any spoon, mind you. This particular spoon was once laced with poison and used to assassinate a lowly noble, his existence a distant memory beneath remembrance of his name. Although his station was modest, puny even, his death was the real reason the Known Lands spiraled into the last great war before our current era of peace. Peng of all Dokkaebi has it, and the temperamental cur refuses to trade."

"I have had my eye on a particular scroll," followed Domeri with a hint of enthusiasm. "It would be the perfect addition to my assortment of final finished works. There was an author long ago, called Shierni, who was famed for his wonderful writing, but eventually he was shamed because he never finished a single work. Beautiful stories, captivating characters, but he completed nothing. The poor sot died penniless and hated. This one scroll, the last thing he ever authored, is a completed work, and would have validated him. Sondyl has the scroll but demands something personally acquired from far away travels. I have tried trading with other Dokkaebi for a fair substitute, but I swear Sondyl has conspired with the whole of Ulburis to shun me."

"Not as bad as Omor, the dried-up lizard wears the item I most wish to add to my collection, a constant mockery," spat Kalem. "He buckles his pants with a button once worn by Lervol, the most famed carnival announcer who audiences loved for his orations at shows of all kinds. The fame led to a somewhat indulgent lifestyle. One day, while bellowing to a crowd, the pressure of his belly overcame the strength of the stitching and the button burst off, hitting an audience member squarely in the eye and dropping his trousers to the ground. Lervol retired that day, never able to recover. There is no other item more perfect for my collection in all of Ulburis. *Ahem*, I gather things that have been used for the last time."

"But if Omor is using the button again, doesn't that mean

the button's use isn't over?" Aeda asked.

"Omor is meaningless, less than insignificant. And besides, once I acquire the button, it will no longer be in use."

"Wouldn't anything you add to your collection by default have been used for the last time?" Aeda questioned with genuine curiosity.

The Dokkaebi's ears twitched. "Silly technicalities, it is about the history and story of the item and who the proper owner was. I have a sword in my collection, used in the last contest of a duelist who lost more duels than any other person in history. Of course, I could pick up that sword and say it is in use again, but would that change the story? The same goes for the button. Its story is with Lervol."

I see now why the Dokkaebi in that caravan were dressed so distinctly. This peculiar individuality is the heart of their existence.

Gieral and Aeda finished their supper and offered cordial goodbyes, retiring to a room reserved expressly for Historians. The outside was lumpy, amorphous limestone, Aeda assuming the lodging would be as pleasant as the dinner. The interior proved her wrong as it was quite cozy with a fire crackling away in the hearth.

There were three beds which could not have been more different. A brightly colored quilt sat atop a rough-sawn wood plank bed. An assortment of furs laid on a masterfully carved poster bed. In the corner of the room, a simple hammock swung. On one wall hung a painting of a bird that looked like a young child created it, while on the opposite wall hung an incredibly detailed pastoral work.

"I have some business to attend to tomorrow," Gieral said,

splashing her face with water over a basin. "You can spend the day roaming the city if you would like. Taphes took you to the mint, but there are still the mines, the foraging caves if you fancy catching a lizard, and many other areas of interest he would be happy to show you. Or you can return to the Market. You already have quite the collection, which some of the Dokkaebi might be interested in."

"How long do you think we'll stay?" Aeda asked, crawling into the hammock.

"At least one more night," Gieral replied, questioningly scanning a towel peppered with holes before using it to dry her face. "When Historians visit cities or towns, the duration of our stay may vary depending on our feelings. Likewise, events outside of our control may pull us in or send us back out. When I first met you, I intended to stay in Biersport for a week."

"I'm sorry for interrupting your plans."

"No need to apologize. The blame lies with the Grey Society. Even then, I don't think either of us would change the result. Remember, sway with the breeze. You will find that even the most concrete, well-organized, infallible plans will often change. Our only obligation is to commune with Runetrees. We should, of course, adhere to local laws and customs, but communing is the focus. Everything else is flexible."

Aeda rested her head on a plush feather pillow, her mind racing with possibilities of what the next morning might bring.

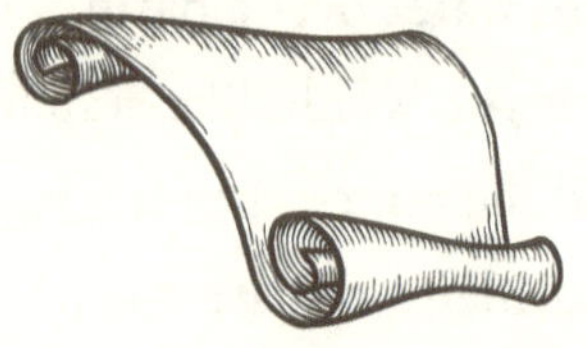

TWENTY-ONE

Aeda woke to the sounds of doors swinging shut, her mentor already gone. In the banquet hall, a bowl of cold dinner leftovers sloshed in her bowl. *How do they find their energy from food like this?* After eating just past the point of hunger, Aeda joined the stream of Dokkaebi flowing into the Market.

Domeri, Kalem, and Arhal tottered through the dense crowd while murmured complaints and hushed irritations filled the air like a thick fog. "Hurry! Could you move slower? Are you aware of the time?" They fussed up to the dais where Domeri lazily flopped open the charter. Arhal pulled back his sleeves and lifted the stylus with a flourish, marking the charter. Leering at the crowd, Kalem yawned. "On this day, Market begins."

It was as if a firecracker went off in a chicken coop. The Dokkaebi screamed and shouted, dashing every which way as covers flew off booths. Aeda eased her way into the throng to seek Peng and the golden spoon. She meandered past countless stalls, reeling at the array of goods—from a piece of driftwood which was vehemently argued over, to a gorgeous crystal vase encrusted with fine gems which was entirely ignored. Pacing down the aisles, she stewed in frustration, unable to find a single golden spoon.

Aeda's spirits lifted on seeing the scrunch-faced Mato. She forced her lips to form a cordial grin and approached the stacks of vile jars.

"Ah, you are back to see old Mato! Change your mind about the pee? I also have some spit from a past Head Librarian somewhere around here, if you might fancy that. It's a surprisingly good quantity." The Dokkaebi's brows raised as he scanned his wares.

"Hello Mato, I was actually wondering if you might help me," she hesitantly replied.

His jovial expression cooled. "How *I* might help *you?*"

"I'm looking for Peng. She has a spoon that Arhal wants, and I'd like to see if I can trade for it."

"Ha!" exclaimed Mato, his smile reappearing. "Starting your own collection? I love when outsiders join in the fun. Oh, oh, don't tell me what you're going for. New collections are so intriguing. Let me guess, hm… you're going after things another Dokkaebi desires for their collection?"

"Er, yes," Aeda replied. *I may as well run with it.*

"Insidious. I love it. I can draw you a little map on this hide. Give me a moment. Anyone else you are looking for?"

"Sondyl and Omor."

"Your day begins with good fortune. I know where those two are as well. Be mindful of Omor though, he has quite a reputation. Not that Peng is the nicest either. Or Sondyl, for that matter. Anyhow, all finished," said Mato after a spurt of furious scribbling. Aeda extended her hand for the hide. "Oh, come now, you didn't think I would just give this to you? This is the Market; items are for trade, not for free."

"You made it in half a moment. It's not like it is some special antique," protested Aeda.

"But it's something you need. Value is driven by desire and necessity, my girl."

"How do I know it's real? Let me see the map. I have plenty to trade for it. I think I have a sample of the Biersport Assembly's wine in here," she bluffed as she patted her satchel. "It's not as if I can memorize a map of an unfamiliar place by looking at it for a second, but I need to be sure I'm not getting a raw deal."

"Fine," he said reluctantly, stretching the map for her to see. Aeda scanned the crude drawing, red circles marking each of the three Dokkaebi. Mato rolled up the map and Aeda promptly turned away.

"Where are you going?" Mato stammered.

"To see Peng," she coyly replied.

"Without the map?"

"I've seen the map. I think I can find my way now."

"You've seen the map and you know where to go?" Mato's face contorted as he tapped a fist on his stall. Spitting out a raspy wheeze, he bowled over in laughter. "Outsmarted by a young Historian visiting Ulburis for the first time. Unthinkable!"

He cheerfully threw the map over the crowd. Aeda leapt off the cart of a passing Dokkaebi, snatching the map between two fingers. Mato's chortling ceased. "Wait! You didn't memorize the map, did you? Fooled once and fooled again!"

Aeda bowed dramatically. "Thank you for the map!" she

cried, departing with a grin on her face and map in hand.

Peng hovered over her stall like an owl searching for mice in a field. There were vases, bowls, spoons, and knives, but neither forks nor plates were in sight. Aeda hoped that the Dokkaebi's reputation was undeserved, but the wishful thought was dashed as Peng crazily swung her arms, driving away a would-be trader before they could even make an offer. Steeling herself, Aeda marched to the stall.

"Hello Peng, I'm Aeda, and I'd like to inquire about a golden spoon."

"And which golden spoon would that be?" Barked the Dokkaebi, waving to a case with stacks of spoons.

"To be blunt, the one that Arhal wants," Aeda nervously replied. *How can I trade with her if this is how she acts when she doesn't even know what I have to offer?*

Peng spat a horrendous, clumpy wad of snot. "I know how badly he wants it, and it brings me great joy knowing he can't bring anything I want. Why should I trade it to you?"

"I'm starting my own collection."

"You want charity?" Sneered Peng.

"No, I want to trade," implored Aeda.

"And? What are you even trying to collect? Whatever shiny pittance you see? That seems to be all people above ground care about."

Irritation at the ill-mannered Dokkaebi rose in Aeda. "I'm looking for objects that others desire, and this spoon is the item I would like to start my collection with. What do you want that

Arhal can't find?"

"What a strange collection. Will you follow others around like a parrot on their shoulder, attempting to outbid them when they mention interest in an item? You starting a collection might be charming to some, but I don't care. It's not as if a child could find what I want, and I don't trade unless I'm getting what I truly want."

Steaming, Aeda breathed deeply. "Try me."

The Dokkaebi glared, an insidious grin peeling across her face. She crawled over the counter, knocking dishes astray. Snatching the golden spoon, she growled her challenge. "Let's see something from beyond the Known Lands."

Trivial, she thinks so little of me that this is the best demand? Aeda retrieved a wooden ring from her satchel, its band topped with a nest of brambles forming a cage for a notably absent gem. Taken from a visiting merchant from across the western seas, she had always fancied the ring and would have worn it herself had the Grey Society not barred Thieves from wearing anything unique or memorable. Peng seized the ring, tossed it between her hands, looped it on the end of a finger, and flicked it to the ground. Aeda scrambled to grab the ring before it was lost among footsteps. Peng was glaring with her arms crossed.

"That ring was from…"

"I don't care. It's dull. Show me something taken from a dead body that has no value for a living person but is important for the dead." Peng put on a show of being bored. She extended an open hand, fingers curling repeatedly while she gazed off to the cavern ceiling.

These can't possibly be genuine requests. Aeda bristled as she dove back through her belongings, finding a square of leather with a brass ring in one corner and a string of numbers stamped in the center. She dropped it into the waiting hand of Peng. The Dokkaebi dangled the square between two nails as if it were a dead rat.

"What is this junk? It's boring."

Aeda yanked the square before Peng could toss it aside. "This is not boring, it's a corpse tag from the morgue of Biersport. It is precisely what you asked for. It's needed for the dead to be properly buried but it's not useful for someone who is alive. Why are you asking for these things if you don't even want them?"

Peng's bitterness eased slightly. "I want a story; you are bringing out objects like rocks from a riverbed. Why should I care about some little wooden ring or a chip of leather? If you hand things over and want me to look at them for what they are without explanation, then I'm going to toss them aside like the garbage they seem to be."

"But you took…"

"What? Don't want the spoon?" The Dokkaebi raised the utensil, her hand clenched like the jaws of a bear trap.

"What do you *actually* want?" Aeda demanded, temples pulsing and teeth clenched.

"I *actually* was looking for something from outside the Known Lands. I also *actually* fancied something taken from a dead body with no use for the living. Those both could have been useful for some trades I have in mind. But I am also in search of an object which was stolen yet is of little value on its own, but in its absence might cause the former owner a significant loss."

Aeda leaned back, puzzling over the bizarrely specific

description. *I stole almost everything in my satchel, that covers the first bit. But why would I steal if I didn't think it was valuable? Worse yet, I pick things I don't think will immediately draw attention. That goes exactly against the last part. What could fit this description?*

Peng grinned and climbed back to her stall, snootily polishing the spoon. Aeda's heart pounded under the pompous gaze of the Dokkaebi. *I refuse to be bested by someone this arrogant.* She opened her satchel, digging through the trinkets until her finger caught a loop of wire. Aeda slowly raised a cloudy blue stone and dangled it in front of the Dokkaebi.

"Go on, what is it?" Said Peng, her interest piqued.

"This," Aeda drawled, "this is a game piece. But not any game piece. I stole this from an Identifier's guards, right from under their noses while they bet huge sums of coin on the game. I took this from the guard who was poised to win. Without it, he would certainly lose instead."

"How did you steal it?" Pressed the Dokkaebi.

"I lifted it from the playing field when they were distracted."

"That bit is obvious. How did you learn to steal?"

"I used to be a Thief."

"A likely story," Peng dismissed.

"It's true, I was a Thief in Biersport!" Aeda's voice was shrill, not appreciating the need to defend the truth that was her former position.

"You expect me to believe you were in the Grey Society?"

"You don't have to believe it, but I was."

"So that's it. A washed-up Thief takes a game piece."

"Not too washed up to steal this," Aeda said indignantly.

"Anything else happen when you took it?"

"I had angered the Identifier."

"Why is that relevant?"

"We were fleeing his sanctuary. Immediately after, Jakro sent the guards I stole from to find us."

"Who is 'we'?"

"My mentor, Gieral, and I."

"Gieral the Historian? She let you steal?"

"She wasn't my mentor yet."

"Hmph." The Dokkaebi eyed the game piece. "It's not much of a story, but it's enough. Give me the stone."

Aeda held the game piece out, clutching it tightly until the spoon was in hand to complete the trade. Brow glistening with sweat, Aeda offered a shaky bow. Peng curiously winked, then hollered at a Dokkaebi who drifted too close to her to display. Spirits raised, Aeda tucked the spoon away and oriented herself to Sondyl and the finished story of the infamously incomplete author.

Dodging an errant club flung into the aisle, Aeda realized the opening frenzy had progressed to a state of anarchy. Through the mania, the oddities and treasures of the Market frequently distracted Aeda. A part of her wanted to abandon her search and trade for enticing curiosities, but she dragged herself away.

Aeda saw Sondyl's stall long before she saw the Dokkaebi. Stacks of shelves and boxes overflowed with books and scrolls; sepia sheets scattered like leaves around a tree in autumn. A scroll lay over the face of a Dokkaebi in a hammock, his arms and legs dangling freely. Aeda tiptoed up, not wanting to disturb his rest. She recoiled as Sondyl's hanging hand swiped at her with a book.

"Whadyawant?" he mumbled, the scroll on his face unmoved.

"You seem relaxed for the Market," Aeda blurted out.

The Dokkaebi snatched the scroll from his head, tossing it to the side in a crumpled pile. Unmoved from his hammock, he squinted at Aeda. "Who are you to tell me about the Market? I'll have you know this is a well-crafted strategy, the unassuming seller and seemingly placid display masking the rare and valuable. Now, what do you want?"

Aeda immediately regretted her blunder. She cleared her throat, speaking as politely as she was able. "I'm Aeda, and I'm starting my collection. I'm gathering items that others desire. I'd like to trade for the only completed work of Shierni."

"Ah, my turn. I'm Sondyl. I have books, trade for one," he mocked. His expression cooled as he spoke again. "You have to work on that opening. Add some fire, some energy, bring a little style. If you don't, I guarantee most Dokkaebi will ignore you, and the ones that do not will be cross because of how dull you sound. The scroll is on the second shelf, to the far right. Take it."

"I've been told that nothing is free in the Market. Why are you giving this to me?"

"Because I want to be free of you. That is the trade. I can tell you are the type to pester me to no end if I don't relent. The persistence of youth exceeds the patience of their elders, or some such like that."

"Domeri said you wanted things acquired from far away travels."

"I came up with that request to bother him. Look behind me. I collect books and scrolls. It does not matter where they came from as long as they are interesting to read. I don't even want that particular scroll; I was holding it to make him squirm for the year. Poor Domeri, it's going to break his heart when he reads that scroll. It's a travesty, an awful waste of paper. Probably for the betterment of the world that Shierni finished nothing else, that scroll is better suited to start a fire than to read."

"So, you're giving it away?" Aeda asked, still dubious about the offer.

"It's growing tiresome having Domeri come by every day, sometimes more than once a day, and now you're here too. I'm not giving it away. I'm trading that scroll for freedom from pests."

Aeda snagged the scroll, not wanting Sondyl to rethink his decision. In the seconds it took to retrieve the writings, Sondyl already had a fresh scroll over his face. She thanked him, scooting away to Omor and the flying button.

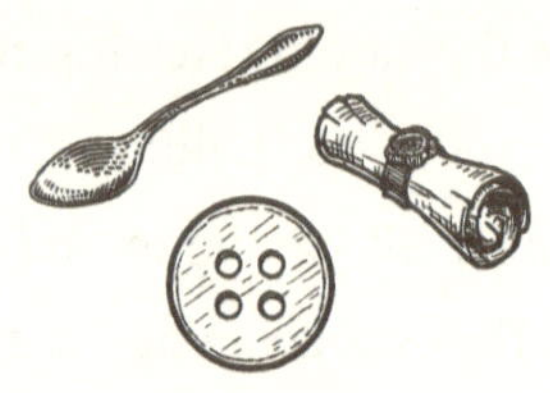

CHAPTER

TWENTY-TWO

Aeda lumbered through the Market under the weight of Peng's and Sondyl's comments, crafting stories for the oddities in her satchel. The sight of Omor flushed the practiced routines from her mind. The Dokkaebi darted back and forth, eyes boring into passersby and harshly judging wares brought before him. On the front of his ochre trousers, held up by olive suspenders, was a rather uninteresting wooden button.

Aeda doubted she had the right Dokkaebi until Kalem sidled over with a bulging bag in tow. Omor tucked his thumbs in his trousers and pushed forward the button in greeting. The Officiant moved to open the bag, but Omor simply snorted. Back and forth, they argued until another Dokkaebi tapped Kalem on the shoulder, ushering her away while Omor laughed.

Aeda puffed her chest and greeted the Dokkaebi. "Hello Omor. I'm Aeda, former Thief of Biersport, Apprentice Historian, and I have come to trade for Lervol's button."

"I don't care who you are, and you certainly didn't arrange for it, so no, you haven't come for it. It is mine and I don't feel like letting it go," Omor spat.

Aeda wiped an errant fleck of saliva from her cheek and steeled herself. "I collect objects that others desire, denying them the addition to their collection forever."

"What does that have to do with anything? I said I am not interested in a trade. Besides, I don't believe your collection for a second. Name one thing you've got that someone else wants. You and all the other above-grounders, always saying they have a satchel of gold fingers when it's got nothing more than a nugget of copper ore."

Aeda smirked knowingly. "I have this spoon, which I'm sure you know Arhal desires above anything else."

"One item does not, a collection, make," challenged Omor.

"Then what of this scroll, the only finished work of Shierni, which Domeri wants so badly?"

"Is it only the two things then, hm? Curious, both the spoon and the scroll are wanted by our lovely Officiants. What else do you have?"

"Now you're playing games. Do you want to keep at this all day as I show you every object I've collected?" She said with a shake of her satchel. "Those are merely a couple of my prized pieces, and they relate to what I came to you for."

"About that," followed Omor, "why should I want to trade with you?"

"If you're trying to keep the button from Kalem, who better to trade with than me? I'm an Apprentice Historian. Once in my hands, the items will be all but gone from Ulburis forever."

The Dokkaebi's face wrinkled, the corner of his left eye twitching. "You mistake my motives. I'm not as vindictive as

Peng. Poor Kalem legitimately cannot provide anything I would want in exchange for this button. It is quite convenient, keeping my favorite trousers together and all. It would take something a little more than the usual for me to trade it away."

Aeda glanced at his stall, home to an incoherent mixture of clothes, armor, and broken charms. "What would you usually trade for?"

"My collection is of objects that people took from someone who tried to harm them," Omor proudly waved.

"Well, Lervol's button doesn't seem to fit in your collection. Are you certain you aren't just having a go at Kalem?"

The Dokkaebi bristled at the insinuation. "The fit of the button matters not. I have it and I like it. Since Kalem wants it badly, it's leverage for me to trade for what I want. Besides, it's not like every item in your possession is a part of your collection, no? Is your, is your bracelet an object that someone else desired?"

Aeda cooled her desire to shout and argue. "Surely Kalem has something you could use to trade for the type of object you want."

"I would rather not. I can get plenty of variety from the Overmarket at my leisure. For this button, I want something more… *personal*." He snarled through jagged teeth. "A young girl such as yourself, you can't possibly have what I want, either. You may as well leave."

Aeda leaned close and whispered. "Are you so sure?"

Not expecting such an assured response, Omor eyed her quizzically. Seizing the moment of opportunity, Aeda overcame her nerves and jumped on an overturned box with a shout. "Come, come if you wish to hear the tale of Melinor, and see if what I have is worthy of a trade!"

"What are you on about?" Omor griped, crossing his arms as a handful of Dokkaebi gathered.

"Come closer. I'll tell you the story of an attempt on my life and you can judge if what I took is worthy of Omor's demands." Aeda leisurely unwound a few silver hairs from the braid at the hilt of her dagger. She looked from face to face of the expectant Dokkaebi. *If they want a story, they'll get a story. I will be as young Melinor in Amrodesa, and there will be no choice but to trade.* As Omor opened his mouth to chide her theatrics, she began her tale. "Not even a week ago, I was sailing with my mentor when we came upon a cave. The water stilled and turned black, the air was cold, not a single bird was singing. We stepped onto a rickety pier and went into the cave, soul cairns crafted with death essences marking our descent into the lair."

Aeda kneeled on the box and the growing audience hushed, squeezing close. "We descended for ages, deep into the cave. Inside was a single, feeble creature."

"What kind of creature?" Asked one Dokkaebi.

"Sh!" hushed a chorus, the Dokkaebi engrossed in the tale.

"It was an old lady, frail and thin, sitting on a rock in the center of a broad room. She was playing an instrument I couldn't see, but the music was gentle, like a trickling creek on a cool morning. My mentor spoke with her, but I couldn't hear their words. I felt the music, like fingers snaking under my skin and into my head, grabbing hold of my hair and moving me like a puppet." Aeda jerked her fingers across her scalp and threw her head back. "A hazy fog masked everything as my hands moved to pick an ancient lock against my will."

"What was the lock to? Couldn't you stop? Quiet!" came the onlookers, Aeda relishing their enthusiasm.

"It was then that I found who, or what, the old lady truly was. In my mind, she called herself Melinor and thanked me for freeing her. Then she stood, a monstrous beast with ten legs, her skin stretched across her bones which poked out all over. She had wrapped her silver hair between the knobs of bone and was plucking them like a lute." Aeda stretched the hair between her fingers and raised it high, strumming with her thumb. "Her true form revealed, the music turned sinister. She lunged at my mentor with nails as long as my hand and as strong as steel. Back and forth they fought while I wrestled with the monster in my mind. She told me in words as clear as the ones I say now, 'soon you will be mine, I will have the life of Gieral and then I will have yours.'"

"What next? How did you stop her? Shut it!"

"I couldn't let it happen. I focused all my energy into breaking free. First, I moved one hand, then the other, and finally I was free. It was barely in time to see her ready to kill my mentor, hands high."

Aeda paused with her hand in the air like a claw, the audience gasping.

"I leaped, dagger out, cutting through her hair." Aeda dropped her hand to draw her dagger, brushing Melinor's hair with a dramatic flourish, as if she had just severed the strands. "Melinor was furious and turned to me. She rose, ready to end my life."

"How did you survive? What about your mentor? Let her finish!"

"Gieral turned and cut the beast down as Melinor's nails brushed against my face. As a prize, I took these strands of her hair, a trophy from the one who attempted to kill me. Now, Omor, do you agree that I have something that might be worthy of trade for Lervol's button?"

The cries of dozens of onlookers filled Omor's ears. He rubbed his chin in contemplation, the corners of his lips faintly curling.

Gieral returned to the Market before closing, spying Aeda feverishly debating a Dokkaebi. She waved and her Apprentice came running over, face flushed and hair astray.

"Were your meetings successful? Did you find out more about the missing Historians?"

"That was a part of it, yes. More than a year has passed since the last sighting of two Historians who frequently travel with the Dokkaebi caravans. It is odd, but they are known to withdraw for long stretches. Their absence is nothing conclusive on its own."

"I don't understand though, why would Historians be disappearing? Who would want that?"

"You have landed on the question that most Historians and Librarians have posed to me when this topic arises. I believe more important than discerning the who or the why is to confirm that members of our order are in fact missing. Until we're certain of what is happening, speculation about motivations of unknown perpetrators is unfortunately unproductive. Anyhow, you look like you have had a busy day. Let's make our way to the banquet. We can beat the rush."

Aeda enthusiastically relayed the essence of her experience in the Market over dinner, tactfully omitting choice details. The caution proved unnecessary as Gieral was distant, responding with cheerful but simple acknowledgement.

That evening Aeda snored in the hammock though Gieral sat awake, brow furrowed as she watched curling wisps of candle smoke.

Aeda slipped out of bed in the morning, surprised to find Gieral still asleep. She tiptoed around the room, gathering her belongings and washing her face as quietly as she was able. After wiping dry with a scratchy towel, Gieral came into view, already dressed and braiding her hair. *How does she do this? And not a single noise? How could I be a Thief for most of my life, a supposed master of quiet and shadow, and I'm completely outdone by her?*

"Well, come on then. From the sound of it, breakfast is already being served," said the humored Historian.

"Do you think we could eat with the Officiants?"

"Depending on their mood, they may allow it. The Officiants are usually willing to accommodate Historians, but we have eaten with them once and you have seen how fickle this group can be."

They chewed on pieces of candied fruit, biding time quietly at the edge of the banquet hall until the Officiants tottered into view. Gieral bowed graciously. "Domeri, Kalem, Arhal, good morning. Might we join you for breakfast?"

"Why not," said Domeri.

"It wouldn't be too much of a bother," echoed Kalem.

"Yes, of course you are welcome to eat with us," encouraged Arhal.

Gieral found their temperament odd, though Aeda simply

shrugged and followed their lead. Over a simple meal of cold root porridge and gelatinous mushrooms, the three Dokkaebi bickered amongst themselves but made space to chat pleasantly with Aeda. As they finished breakfast, she presented a bold request.

"May we join you on the dais today when you open the Market?" She asked, honey sweet. "I have so enjoyed learning about your customs."

The three Dokkaebi looked nervously amongst themselves.

"It would be unusual," said Arhal, "but I don't see a reason why you can't. There are no rules against it."

"No rules against it," mimed Domeri.

"Perhaps this once," added Kalem.

Gieral shot an inquisitive look to Aeda, who smiled in reply and planted herself beside the Officiants.

They passed through the Market, the Dokkaebi so focused on haranguing the Officiants they hardly noticed the Historian and her Apprentice. Aeda clasped her hands to quell their shaking as they ascended the steps. The view from the dais was breathtaking. The bright eyes of a sea of Dokkaebi illuminated within the shimmering glow of the cavern.

Gieral stood aside, giving ample berth to avoid disturbing the proceedings. Counter to her mentor, Aeda marched over to the Officiants as Kalem retrieved the runed orb. Domeri clamped the charter shut, an audible groan echoing from thousands of waiting Dokkaebi.

"Aeda, what are you doing?" Gieral hissed.

Aeda ignored her mentor. "Domeri, please open the charter again."

"Aeda, this is too much," interjected Gieral, more flustered than when she lay beneath Melinor's claws. "My apologies for my Apprentice."

"Don't apologize for me, I'll apologize myself if I'm in the wrong," Aeda ripped. She turned back to the quivering Dokkaebi. "We traded, and if I recall the agreement was that at a time of my choosing, you would open the charter for me until read."

"Now is not a good time," Domeri clasped the charter tight to his chest.

Arhal and Kalem ogled at their compatriot. Eyes wide, they spoke in unison. "You traded with *her*?"

"We explicitly agreed that it would be a time of my choosing," said Aeda, rejecting Domeri's complaint.

He grumbled and coughed down his words. "Hm, yes, what harm can come from her taking a peek at the charter? It needs to be opened, anyway."

The clamoring of the crowd eased at the opening of the tome. Arhal's complexion paled. Aeda continued unwaveringly. "Arhal, please ready your stylus. Our agreement, if I recall, was for you to write five words of my choice at a time of my request."

Domeri gaped at Arhal. "By the blessed branches of Namuor, you complain about me opening a tome and you agree to write words for her? I am doing nothing more than opening the charter. How could you agree to write?"

"Well, it wouldn't have been a problem if you weren't fool enough to open the charter! Why should I believe she would ask for me to write in the charter, of all places?"

"Are you sure of what you are doing, Aeda?" Gieral cautioned. "This is a permanent act, not a trifle, and what you do now will forever be a part of Dokkaebi history."

"You shouldn't be hasty," wheezed Kalem. She shrank into her robes, sweating profusely.

"Yes, please listen to your mentor," begged Arhal.

Aeda's brow furrowed. "Gieral, you said that everything we do is a part of history. Isn't writing things down merely a formality of an idea? And to you three. They were all fair trades, were they not? Or are you going to explain to all of Ulburis how you won't honor our trades?"

Arhal tugged at his sleeves, fibers fraying between his trembling fingers. "What am I to write?"

Aeda whispered in his ear, and his eyes nearly popped out of his head. "What? Are you sure?"

"Yes."

"Positive?"

"Yes."

"Certain you don't want something different?"

"Yes."

"What about…"

"Arhal, I'm sure." Aeda stood back as the crowd roared, enraged by the delay.

"A trade is a trade," he sighed in resignation, marking the charter.

Anticipation brewed and all of Ulburis demanded action. "Read it! Start the trades!" came their cries. Kalem let out a guttural wheeze as she tried to laugh at the other Officiants. She silently conceded and walked to the open charter. Her face drooped and her hands shook. Arhal and Domeri looked incredulously at their fellow Officiant, too embarrassed to say anything further.

Face down, Kalem turned to the rambunctious crowd. The Dokkaebi hushed. Her voice bellowed mightily. "Aedreana… is…" She faltered, squinting to confirm what she was about to say. She meekly squeaked the final words. "The Dokkaebi Queen?"

A dreadful silence filled the cavern, prompting even the Ogres to pause their work. Sweat ran from Aeda's forehead to her cheek and her heart beat faster than the night of the brigand ambush. *What have I done?*

From the back of the dais came a strained snicker. Gieral could not hold back her amusement and her laughter echoed over the Market. Moments later, Mato joined with a hearty chuckle. The whole of Ulburis roared, jeering at the Officiants and cheering Aeda's cleverness as their cackles spread like a fire through a bed of dried leaves.

The thoroughly astounded and alarmed Officiants threw their hands in the air and abandoned the day's opening ceremony. Aeda froze, uncertain what to do now that her plan had come to fruition. She bit her lip and stood awkwardly until Gieral guided her to the stairs. "It would seem that your subjects would like to meet you, my queen."

"I'm sorry for yelling at you," Aeda said sheepishly, while trying to maintain her conviction.

"As Iyra, you apologize for the wrong thing. You hatched quite the plan. Perhaps it would be good to share at least a little of it with me next time. Then again, I can see why you might not want to, as I would certainly have tried to stop you. Let us call it even. I almost got you killed in Melinor's cave, and you have now repaid the favor by almost killing me with shock."

"I don't think they're quite the same and I saved you from the runewriter too," Aeda rebutted.

"Yes, and you also stole from me, which I rewarded by offering you a place as my Apprentice," countered Gieral.

"I would say we're even as well."

A deafening ovation greeted them at the base of the steps. Like a parade, Dokkaebi flooded the banquet halls to celebrate their new queen. It was the first time in more than a generation that the Market had not opened, yet not a single Dokkaebi was upset.

The Dokkaebi had constructed an impromptu throne for Aeda to sit upon, a wobbly platform of stacked tables. Climbing up steps of staggered chairs, Gieral motioned for Aeda to sit at the head of the top table. Domeri, Kalem, and Arhal were pushed up while Aeda waved for Taphes, Mato, Omor, Peng, and Sondyl to join them. Dokkaebi drank from mugs filled with ale and goblets of fruit wine, as the room buzzed with laughter at Aeda's masterful deceit.

To celebrate their new queen, the Dokkaebi cooked with fervor. Foods of every kind were prepared, flavored with rare ingredients acquired from the Overmarket. The aromas rivaled those of the Great Library as platters flowed out, laden with the tempting morsels. Charred peppers topped grilled pheasants, sweet herb coated loins and legs of goat roasted over spits, innards and chops and leafy, sour herbs fried in deep pots of oil. Vegetables were steamed, broiled, and sauteed with the most exotic of spices. The center of each table housed a mountain of bread, sliced in thick slabs and drizzled with scented oils.

For hours upon hours, through the day and into the night,

to a time past any reckoning, the Dokkaebi ate and danced and sang, banging the tables and chanting about their queen. Aeda joined in every bit of the festivities, spinning and cheering and laughing as though she were a Dokkaebi herself.

Above ground, perplexed merchants waited in the Overmarket for the entire day as the Dokkaebi never appeared.

CHAPTER

TWENTY-THREE

Aeda woke to a bump on the bottom of her foot. She sleepily drew her knee up to her chin, nearly tumbling from the hammock. Aeda grumbled at Gieral, who was twirling a ladle with a ridiculously long handle. "Is this some sort of sick initiation rite? Why do you wake so early every day?"

"I know it was hard work celebrating, but, my highness, you need to get up at some point. Days don't wait for us to rise; they begin on their own and it is on us to be there to experience them."

"Is it wrong to want to experience the day a little later, or maybe experience more of it from a bed?" Aeda complained.

"We have business to attend to this morning. Before we leave Ulburis, it is time for you to fulfill your duty as a Historian and commune with the Runetree."

Aeda lazily rolled out of the hammock and gathered her belongings. "Not overstaying our welcome?"

"Especially so with the fanfare yesterday."

"You aren't angry about what I did?"

"I'm not here to judge you. As your mentor, I'm here to guide you. You are still your own person, and your decisions are your own. I'm of the belief that Historians should not get more involved than absolutely necessary, but that is my belief. As long as your actions do not defy your duties as a Historian, who am I to say what is allowed or not? And between us, I never imagined that the Dokkaebi kitchens could produce such food. Speaking of the kitchens, I went for a walk and they're already pulling out the spores and salamanders. Not to say that is a cause for leaving, but it certainly is not a reason to stay."

"Why don't you immediately commune with the Runetree when you arrive in a city or a town?"

"That is a matter of preference. For some Historians, a trip to the Runetree first is their habit. I find value in time spent among the residents, gauging the climate of the populace to give myself a feeling for how the winds are blowing. Communing is also a nice way to culminate my visit. As a timely example, we will now record your coronation, which would have been missed had we communed on arrival."

Gieral proved to be unfortunately right about breakfast, an overly generous portion of mealy spore porridge with chunks of cured salamander ladled over cold remnants from the prior day's banquet. A few early-rising Dokkaebi greeted Aeda, providing a welcome distraction from the slop filling her bowl.

Gieral led through an inconspicuous opening in the monstrous pillar at the center of Ulburis. Slick, narrow steps were barely lit by glowing blue lichens clinging to the walls. Gieral marched on comfortably, sharing a piece of candied fruit.

Aeda lost count of steps and minutes, the sweet long gone

by the time they spilled into a cavernous room. The Runetree, unlike any plant Aeda had seen, grew down from the bulbous ceiling, a tangle of intricately curled brown roots which spread above and extended to the floor, strands hovering in the air like outstretched hands. All along its limbs were bursts of bright pink and green mosses and drooping white mushrooms shining radiantly. Purple and grey runes enrobed the Runetree, emitting a soft lavender light.

Gieral kneeled by the core of the Runetree, then Aeda followed suit. Her mentor gently gripped her tome and brought her stylus to her chest. She guided a stream of soul fragments to the tome's cover, then to the Runetree. The book levitated above her hand and opened. Plum runes with dashes of pink flowed from the Runetree to the turning pages of the Gieral's tome. Aeda beamed when she repeated the ritual and her tome rose to accept runes from the Dokkaebi Runetree.

For a few minutes, they sat in quiet meditation, recording the history of Ulburis. Gieral's tome stilled, and she elegantly secured its clasp. A moment later, Aeda came out of her trance with a shudder. Her tome slipped to the floor, and she clambered after it, mindfully securing it to her belt.

"That was your first official act as a Historian," said Gieral. "And done as queen of the city, no less."

From Thief to Queen of the Dokkaebi… and I stand here, with a purpose, beside a mentor who actually cares about my existence. I wonder what Braedyn would think if he could see me now. Well, he probably wouldn't care. But the other Thieves… could they imagine how far I've come? Thoughts drifting, Aeda eyed Gieral's tome, clad in rich brown leather with a blue-grey hue. Unimaginably intricate decorations of leaves and branches and roots covered its entire surface.

"When will my tome look like yours?" Aeda asked, wiping a smudge from the smooth tan cover of her own tome.

Gieral looked to the tomes with fascination and a smile. "You will see the change in your tome the day you stop looking at it."

Will she ever speak clearly?

Gieral led to the elevators, Aeda trudging behind. She sighed and joined Gieral in a shuttle, ruefully pulling the lever. Catapulted up through the cavern, the Dokkaebi city grew distant in a blink.

A brisk, grey morning darkened the empty Overmarket. Gieral went to a cluster of inns and stables at the edge of the market to retrieve her horse and mule, brought by couriers from Amrodesa. Aeda visited a messenger, a groggy woman with hair hanging over her face. She took a rolled letter from the Apprentice and tied it to the leg of a pigeon with a blue cap. A runeword enveloped the bird with grey wisps, and it flew off, destined for the Great Library.

Aeda took a last look at the Overmarket and was greeted by a gaggle of Dokkaebi, Taphes and Mato front and center. She shared hugs, and the Dokkaebi offered her parting gifts, from a patina coated bronze ring to a perfectly round lump of copper the size of a pea to a tiny vial from Mato, the contents of which she thought best not to know. Overwhelmed by their kindness, Aeda thanked them until the sun edged above the hills and Gieral started towards the road.

Aeda gave a final bow and followed to the rim of the Overmarket where a green vale filled with lush trees with pink tipped leaves stretched out to the horizon. Although Aeda knew she would dearly miss being among the Dokkaebi, she was tingling with excitement. Aeda marched forward and took the lead, Gieral smiling as the sun rose behind them.

EPILOGUE

The four moons rose over a village of quaint huts topped with layered frond roofs, sitting on stilts above a shallow river. The enclave was tucked between sky-scraping mountains and an arid desert. Children splashed and giggled in the water while their parents relaxed in the cool evening breeze.

Inside one dwelling, a man leaned over a desk illuminated by a white candle sitting on a blackened iron dish. His hair was a blend of greys and wheat-browns, reflecting his transition into the latter part of middle age. A trim beard framed his narrow face, skin weathered and wrinkled. He wore simple cloth shoes below slim, tan woven pants and a loose cream shirt extending to his knees. Before him were three leather-bound tomes with metal chains strung through the spine. Burned runes filled the open pages as if they had been branded like cattle.

A knock sounded.

"Please, come in," said the man to the lithe figure standing in the doorway, his voice mild and welcoming.

The woman's curly red hair flowed atop her shoulders. Leather boots clopped as she strode over and dropped two tomes on the table. The man looked at his guest, noting a scar on her arm in the final stages of healing.

"Gently, please," he requested. "Remember, these tomes are sacred. We must be respectful."

"My apologies," responded the woman, coarse yet still sincere.

Tears welled in the man's eyes as he gingerly oiled the binding of the tomes. "It is alright. Though perhaps we should talk about Gieral. Your decision to approach her was… unfortunate."

The woman placed a hand over her scar. "There are whispers from our sources. Everywhere she goes, she asks about missing Historians."

"Her queries are not of consequence."

"But what if her suspicions are confirmed?"

"I have complete faith in the thoroughness of you and your compatriots. Besides, I doubt there is enough time for her to move beyond a mere hunch."

"Do you have all you need?"

"We are close now, very close."

Brendan Corbett was raised in a southern, Korean, military family, and as a child, he moved more than a dozen times. His professional career has followed a similarly roving path, from job shop operator to industrial engineer to nonprofit director, and now to his love of writing.

Through all these experiences, books were a constant source of escape and adventure, leading him to craft a series about an outcast finding their place in the world.

You are welcome to connect with Brendan at https://www.authorbrendancorbett.com/.